Saving Lisa

E. L. BOYER

First printing 2024
www.boyersbookshelf.com
liz@elboyer.com

Sogale Books LLC.
ISBN Paperback 979-8-9884029-5-4

FORWARD AND ACKNOWLEDGEMENTS

S tatistics taken from the US government website state, '*Of the 731 foreign national adults certified in 2022, 11 percent were sex trafficking victims, 73 percent were labor trafficking victims, 14 percent were both victims of sex and labor trafficking, and 2 percent with the form of trafficking in persons unspecified to HHS.*'

The article was found on the internet titled <u>2023 Trafficking in Persons Report: United States</u>; subtitle: <u>Office To Monitor and Combat Trafficking In Persons.</u>

It is a long report with many statistics, recommendations, and safety tips. Bottom line: Sex trafficking is a severe problem in the US and the world. I am not an expert by any means, but I know one thing: this was not a 'THING' just a few short years ago.

I want to thank Katie Clancy for her generous time as my beta reader. Fortunately for me, she has an excellent eye for detail, which is critical as an RN. I, too, was an RN, but I am now retired and enjoying every minute of it. God Bless all healthcare workers. They are caring and kind; I am proud I was one of them.

The FBI agent Jay Camp was created to honor dear friends who lost their youngest son in 2023 at the age of 43. His name was Jay Combs, Jr. It was unexpected. Although I had never met him, I understood him to be a super father and husband. I wanted to give him a place in my book and my heart.

I hope you enjoy the story, but more importantly, that you learn about this country's problems with trafficking in many forms.

E. L. Boyer

chapter

1

Jeffrey Edwards was pacing his spacious suite in the largest office building in downtown Raleigh. He was in a dilemma and needed to talk with Britt, his friend and partner, about the venture they started three years ago. It had proved quite lucrative, but now he felt the noose tighten. They had gone into business with an unsavory character he met when in New York City on business. One evening, he was approached in the hotel's lobby by a man who introduced himself as 'Cobbler.' He asked him where he was from, and when Jeffrey told him he was near Raleigh, NC, the man invited him to join him in the hotel's lounge later that evening.

Jeffrey asked for his real name when he met him later that night. Cobbler said, "I don't give my real name for reasons you don't need to know."

Jeffrey told him he didn't think he wanted to be in business with someone who wouldn't give his real name.

"Let me tell you about it, then you can decide, yes?" asked Cobbler.

Once he told Jeffrey what kind of business it was, he asked if he would like to join. Jeffrey, always interested in a new venture, asked him more about it. He was thinking about Britt Clayton and told Cobbler he had a friend he thought would like to join him in such a venture. Cobbler told him the money was lucrative and did not take much time. "I'm sure a businessman like you could find someone to do the bidding for you."

"Luring prostitutes to get off the streets and work on the party ships?" asked Jeffrey.

"It's not that difficult. They are treated with respect, and many beg to stay even when their time is up. I've been at this for eight years and have had no complaints," Cobbler assured him.

"How do you ensure there is no law enforcement lurking around?"

"It all takes place on moving vessels, mostly yachts, and virtually no one checks yachts," Cobbler told him.

Jeffrey knew that was true. To search a ship like a home, they would need a warrant to board the ship, and a warrant would be challenging to get with a traveling vehicle. Jeffrey agreed to the venture. He would call Britt when he returned home to see if he was interested.

He and Cobbler shook hands, and that sealed his agreement. Cobbler didn't like paper trails. He told Jeffrey not to worry about the payment. Jeffrey would need to set up a separate bank account with an innocuous name, like a shell account, and then give Cobbler the account number. Funds would be deposited by wire in increments that would not raise eyebrows.

"Don't worry; we'll work out the details later. Let me know when you're ready to start, and it will all be explained."

When Jeffrey returned to Raleigh, he had lunch with Britt and told him about the chance meeting and opportunity. Britt readily agreed since Jeffrey had worked out a plan.

"My children are in braces and private schools. It gets expensive," Britt told him.

Jeffrey began the venture by using Vinnie, his fixer, to lure the pros to a hotel and then take them to the boat. Once aboard, they were told they would be servicing johns up and down the coast. Jeffrey had used Vinnie in other more sensitive ventures, so he was a trusted employee. In his mind, he was assisting in getting the girls into a safer environment.

Cobbler had never complained about his selections. Instead, he gave Jeffrey and Britt bonuses at the end of the year. "A Christmas bonus," he called it. Jeffrey read accounts of what these operations did with the women. He heard they were forced to stay in prostitution until they paid off their keep. The problem was that they never paid it off. Cobbler kept perfect records of each woman and what they required. They were well-fed and had healthcare, and if needed, an abortion would be performed. The girls were taking birth control, but accidents happened.

Recently, Jeffrey received a call from Cobbler, who said he was becoming pressured to procure younger girls.

"How much younger?" Jeffrey asked.

"You know, underage. My clients are requesting prepubescent girls or, minimally, already in puberty. I know it doesn't please you to hear this. You were more comfortable with only prostitutes because they were easier to attract. I understand if you are uncomfortable with it, and I will find another source. With the open border, many dark web sites were overflowing with children."

Jeffrey was taken by surprise. The police were on high alert for human trafficking, and there was talk that the legislature was considering a law to give law enforcement more tools to help them find underage girls and boys who are being sex trafficked. That would hurt the possibility of getting what the johns wanted. He wasn't sure if it was worth it. He knew he would need to meet with Britt soon.

He told Cobbler, "I'll contact you when I talk with my partner. You are asking a lot in this heavily policed area."

"Okay, no problem, but don't take too long. We have movement happening soon in your area."

"What do you mean?" asked Jeffrey.

"We have started using shipping containers, as opposed to yachts. There are fewer restrictions, and the cargo can be hidden more easily. I know that sounds harsh, but it is what it is. A vessel will leave New York in about a week. It will take almost a week to get to your area, so time is of the essence. Let me know if you can't or don't want to, and we will make other arrangements."

"I'll talk with my partner and reply in a few days. Soon enough?" asked Jeffrey.

"I can live with that." Cobbler hung up.

Jeffrey Edwards was considered a brilliant hedge fund manager. He graduated third in his class at Wharton School of Business. His goal was not to work at all, but circumstances changed that. He grew up in a wealthy family on Long Island, New York. His father was a sought-after criminal attorney with many clients in the mob.

During the 1990s, the newly elected Federal District Attorney of the Southern District of New York in the late 1980s, Rudy Giuliani, was on a mission to get the mob out of New York, and he waged war against the five major crime families. Eventually, Jeffrey's father had fewer and fewer clients that paid well. He was still a well-known criminal attorney until he died in 2010, but his status gradually dwindled, as did his income. He was also somewhat of a ladies' man and spent lavishly on his escorts, including trips to Las Vegas. Jeffrey's mother was a long-suffering housewife who loved her husband and her only son and never complained. She died in 2012 of a broken heart, thought Jeffrey. The doctor called it heart failure.

Jeffrey loved both of his parents and appreciated that his father provided well for him and his mother and afforded him a good education. He never wanted for anything. When he turned sixteen, his father bought him a new car. He always had a fashionable wardrobe. His parents took him to Europe, The Bahamas, and several cruises, too many to count. His family was small; his mother had been an only child, and her parents were deceased.

His father had three brothers. Only one of them married happily and had a family. Jeffrey knew his two cousins who lived in Vermont.

He rarely saw them. They invited him to their vacation house to go skiing, but it wasn't his thing, so he put them off by telling them he was busy at work. He golfs occasionally, and that was about all he was good at as far as sports goes. He enjoyed watching football and baseball and had his favorite teams, which he bet on weekly.

In the meantime, he knew he needed to get home early tonight because his wife wanted to go to the symphony. He married a trophy wife who liked to be seen at high-society functions. He didn't mind too much, however. She was gorgeous, but unfortunately for him, they had lackluster sex; ever since their honeymoon, she showed no interest. He had taken care of that one problem by enjoying a variety of companions regularly.

One of his favorites was due any minute, so he should make it home in time to go with his wife to the symphony. His assistant rang his intercom and told him the next appointment had arrived. "Send her in, please."

He walked to the door and greeted Katarina, locking the door behind her. He had no desire to get caught in a compromising position. After all, his clients deserved his utmost attention. His time with Katarina was special. He met her in New York on one of his trips before he married. They had a sexual interlude while he was there, and he never forgot her.

She moved to the Raleigh area, and he found her again at one of the strip clubs. She said she had no family here and left Russia for New York City to escape the Oligarchs, but unfortunately, she told him, the Russian Oligarchs found her in New York and were demanding and cruel to her. She was afraid they would find a way to return her to Russia, so she decided to move, and Raleigh was where she ended up. He assured her he would never be cruel but would like to have her to himself, and he would allow her to continue at her other job if she so desired. She stayed at the club but never went out with anyone else. She was loyal to only him. He put her in an apartment and bought her nice clothes and jewelry.

Once, he took her on a trip with him after he was married. His wife wasn't interested in going to Vegas, but Katarina was; he wanted to test her loyalty. There was a friend of his that went along with his ruse. He was from Russia but had been Americanized and preferred American women. He asked him to flirt with Katarina one night in the Casino to see if he could get her in his room. He failed miserably and lost $10k in the meantime. Jeffrey was happy to hear that Katarina refused his advances. He wrote his friend a check for $10k and gave Katarina his Gold American Express to shop in any store she wished. She picked Gucci. Lucky him.

After that, he never tested her again and gave her anything she wanted. His sexual desires were always sated whenever he was with her. He happily went home to his trophy wife and went to the symphony. They enjoyed a night out in a club with her best friend, whom he had slept with a few times. Once home, his wife feigned a headache and went to bed after doing her fancy nightly face ritual. *I am so glad Katarina came today. I can dream of her tonight, he mused to himself...*

chapter

2

Ally Malcom was on her way to her catering job in Leland; it started around six, and she was due to be there by five. She was running into more traffic than usual, probably with people getting off work, but also, the area was growing by leaps and bounds. She was anxious to discover how Gene's time with his cousin went. Gene owned Three Island Catering, where she worked for the better part of two years. He told her he was an only child and never knew anything about his family. His mom raised him; he never knew his father. His mother was estranged from her family for reasons he was never told.

Ally encouraged him to look into his family heritage by doing a simple DNA test with one of the major companies. She had spoken with him briefly, and he told her he had discovered he had some cousins, one of whom lived close by and was planning a get-together.

Just recently, she had helped her friend Mary find out how her late husband's aunt had disappeared over fifty years ago. Mary's son had done a DNA test and discovered a first cousin he never knew about. It answered many questions that they were still processing. It was a well-known case in the Atlanta area, and now that they understand she didn't meet with foul play, her friend, Mary Hughes, planned to go to the Atlanta police with the information. She hoped to go with her on the trip since she and Mary had worked so hard on it together. They were still working on the when and how.

The catering tonight was for a fiftieth wedding anniversary. She assumed the couple must be wealthy because of where the event was held. The celebration was in an exclusive golf community clubhouse, where you were expected to have a sponsor to be able to join. She had heard that from other people. Sara, Three Island Catering's office manager, told her they expected around a hundred people.

When she arrived, she spotted Gene's large van with the catering kitchen being towed. She waited as he carefully parked so it would be easier for the staff to unload. When he was done, she walked over and greeted him. "It's been a while. Did you enjoy your time with your 'new family'?" she asked him.

"I sure did. My cousin couldn't have been nicer; we hit it off immediately. She arranged for two other cousins to come with their families. One lives in Blaylock County and owns a large excavation company. It's a big operation. The other lives in Raleigh and is a dentist. Can you believe it?"

"That is great, Gene; I'm glad you could connect. Now you'll have people you can send Christmas cards to and all kinds of things. Did any of them need a kidney?" Ally was still kidding him about the positive things about having relatives when he first sent off his DNA kit. She loved that he took her advice.

"Sure, sure. Just wait until it's your turn, Ally."

"Have you told your mother yet?"

"Yes, I told her about the get-together and that she was invited, but she begged off. She didn't think it would be appropriate for her to show up after all these years. You know how people can be. My cousin was disappointed that she didn't feel she would be welcome. Sometimes, you have to let bygones be bygones. She was the only one left out of seven children. It was a long story with many twists and turns. You know how families can be. One of these days, we will discuss it over a few drinks. Sounds good?"

"Yes, it does. I have a few I can share with you, too!"

She went into the clubhouse and started helping Eliza set up the tables. The couple had a son and two daughters who were also there to assist. The setup went quickly because they already had a whole side of the clubhouse with tables and photos of their parents from their wedding and their children's and grandchildren's lives over the years. It was tastefully done, Ally thought as she admired the images, and she wondered how many years her parents had been married. *It must be coming up on sixty*, she thought.

She made a mental note to check with Janet, her sister, to see if they should start planning a celebration. They had a small get-together for their fiftieth, but it was a small event since they had just moved to Bartow shortly before that and had yet to meet many people. They had an active social life now, so she thought they would want a much larger celebration the next time.

Neal, her boyfriend, was expected down this weekend. They planned a fall trip to Asheville with her friend Mary and her boyfriend. She wanted to visit The Biltmore House and The Billy Graham Museum. She had been dating Neal, an anesthesiologist in Chapel Hill, for over two years. It was hard to believe she had been in NC that long. The pandemic was over, well, at least the worst part of it. She refused to take the vaccine while working in Manhattan as an RN and ultimately lost her job.

She had been an RN for thirty years and had always complied with her employer's yearly demands for the flu shot. When the pandemic hit New York, she had taken care of some of the worst cases and saw many people die without being able to see their loved ones. The medical staff and all hospital employees were exposed for months before the vaccine became available. She knew it was a virus, and she had been exposed, so that meant she had developed antibodies. She hadn't been sick yet, so when the vaccine became available, she decided she didn't need it.

Her employer followed the CDC guidelines and mandated that anyone who worked there be vaccinated, hence her dismissal. Therefore, she left New York and moved into her grandmother's beach house. It was left to her mother when her grandmother passed. No one else in the family was interested, so her mother allowed her to live there. She was slowly renovating it.

She and her friend Mary met shortly after she moved to North Carolina. One afternoon, Mary showed up with a casserole in hand, and they broke bread and had a bottle of wine with it. A friendship was born, and they had been close friends ever since. Mary was a sounding board when she was trying to help the Morgans solve their daughter's mysterious disappearance. She had only been in the beach house a couple of weeks when she saw on the news that a human skeleton had washed up on a beach relatively close to where she lived.

When she found out the remains were those of a student she had gone to school with thirty years before, she was shocked. When she realized Katie's parents lived nearby, she contacted them. She became close to Katie Morgan's parents through one of the saddest times of their lives. She was glad she had spent the time to help them discover how their daughter died. They could piece most of the mystery together, but there were still many questions to which they would never find the answers.

Her friend, Mary, as it turned out, had a mystery of her own. Her now-deceased husband's aunt disappeared in 1965. They found a reporter who wrote an article about the case almost fifteen years after the disappearance, and he had heard from a man who claimed he was Mary's private investigator for a while. It was full of intrigue, and they won't ever know why, but she staged her disappearance. Through DNA, Mary's son inadvertently found a name in the family tree he was unfamiliar with, so he contacted his mother, Ally's friend, and they learned it was Michael Collins, the son of Mary Hartwell, Tom's aunt, who had disappeared. Everything came full circle, and they were able to piece together much of the mystery.

By seven o'clock, the party was in full swing. A trio of musicians played popular tunes of the sixties. The crowd was dancing, and everyone seemed to be having fun. After serving dessert, Gene sent the crew in to begin cleaning up. Ally stayed to help; although it wasn't in her job description, she liked to give them a hand. Gene told her she could leave once they were ready to pack up and leave. "I'll see you on Thursday for the big birthday party in North Myrtle," said Gene.

"Yes, you will, and I cannot wait."

Ally's friend, Marie Morgan, was throwing her husband Larry a 75th birthday party, and Three Island Catering was catering it. Ally was looking forward to meeting Katie's two brothers and their families. She had heard so much about them from Marie. She was invited as a guest, but she wanted to take part in helping the catering team.

"It will be my pleasure," she told Marie.

She planned to stay afterward and party as long as she could hold out. Mary and her boyfriend, Roger, also planned to be there.

chapter

3

"Missy, come here, girl." Cynthia was taking her dog to the groomer that morning. She usually loved to go, so she didn't know why she wasn't coming when she called. She walked around her sizeable colonial-style home and realized she was closed up in the office. "Silly girl," she said to Missy as she picked her up and stroked her back. "We do that all the time, don't we?"

After Missy was groomed, Cynthia planned to take her to her son's house so her granddaughters could keep her company. She was going to Raleigh tomorrow and didn't want her to be alone all day. She loved her grandchildren, all girls, and knew she was lucky to have them. She could only have one child, a son, but would have loved more children.

During her lifetime, Cynthia Curtis had been a banner of causes. She remembered when the abortion bill, otherwise known as Roe vs. Wade, was first passed by the Supreme Court. She marched against it with her mother. It was her mother's cause, and she remembered all the hula-bub as a small child. She had since taken up the cause of getting the Supreme Court to strike it down. Thankfully, she and all of her other passionate pro-lifers won that case. She was fully aware that it wasn't over. It was now up to the states to pass laws regarding the practice. She thought North Carolina's law was reasonable. She wanted a complete ban but accepted the reality of the times. "Pick your battles," her mother would always say. Unfortunately, she had learned there were too many battles.

Her most recent one was the trafficking of minors. Technically, it was all human trafficking, but the children were her main cause. She had several meetings with the legislature members in helping to pass a Bill to give law enforcement more tools to find trafficked children and rescue them. She had been successful in getting it passed in the House. She felt good about the Senate passing it, but her inner voice told her not to leave anything to chance.

Her passions go way back to when she was about four years old. They would visit her grandmother in upstate New York during the summer. Her mother grew up there, then went south for college at William and Mary. She had her sights on becoming a teacher. She would have, except she met her future husband and went a different way. But before that, injustices framed her whole life, and it was in her own family.

She discovered that her mother's brother had been wrongly accused of an armed robbery in their small town of Eula. It turned out that he resembled another man who was notoriously bad and lived in the town next to them. It was too late by the time they figured it out. Her uncle served five years in prison for that crime, which ruined him. People never believed he was innocent even though the other man confessed to the crime. Her grandmother became a crusader for wrongly imprisoned men and women. She was a forerunner of the Innocence Project programs that were now popping up nationwide. The problem then, of course, was that DNA had not yet been discovered. It was many years before a blood test could exonerate someone. She worked on local cases where she could drive to and return in a day. By the time she died, they say she was responsible for getting at least a half dozen people out of jail, including one pregnant woman who became pregnant by the rapist whom she killed in self-defense. She was proud of her grandmother.

Cynthia's mother somewhat fell in her footsteps, but she married a lawyer, who became a judge. She could do only so much without jeopardizing her husband's career.

Cynthia went farther south and graduated from the University of North Carolina at Chapel Hill. Her major was history, and she dreamed of becoming a college professor. However, the man she married became a lawyer and also had his sights on a judgeship but never made it because he was struck down by cancer.

Luther Curtis was the love of Cynthia's life. She probably would have been an old maid if she had not met and married Luther. He swept her off of her feet, literally. She was coming out of the library at the campus one afternoon and was looking at a pamphlet she had just picked up about a rally to help Ethiopians when she bumped into a student coming up the steps who was looking at a schedule of classes. They ran into each other, and both fell on the steps. She was so embarrassed, and so was he. They started apologizing to each other, and then there was a spark. She fell in love with his husky good looks and his deep brown eyes. He wasn't the type she thought she would fall in love with, making it much more exciting. He asked her to go to the corner coffee shop, and she accepted. They drank only one cup but sat and talked for two hours. The coffee shop didn't mind; they welcomed people to come in and relax.

They were only able to have one child, a son, Martin. He had made them both so proud. He married a wonderful girl, and they had three precious little girls, the joys of her life. She visited them often and hoped to have at least one of them follow in her footsteps as an advocate for the oppressed. One of them could become a lawyer and then even a judge. Luther would be so proud.

She took Missy to the groomer, whom she had used for many years. "Hello, Daphne. Missy is ready to see you." Cynthia held Missy out so Daphne could take her, and Missy licked Daphne on the cheek, her way of saying hello.

"I love you, too, baby," said Daphne.

"Call me when she is ready. She's going to spend the night with the grands tonight. I am going to Raleigh tomorrow to take care of business and didn't want her to be alone all day."

"I will, Miss Cynthia. See you later."

Missy walked over to the crate prepared for her until it was ready for her turn. She knew the ropes since she had been here every two weeks her entire life. Cynthia was on her way to get her manicure and pedicure when she received a call from Senator Willis. "Hello, Shelbourne," she said when she answered the phone.

"Are you coming up today?" he asked her.

"I was planning on in the morning. Why, what's up?"

"There's nothing that can't wait until tomorrow. I just had a couple of senators having second thoughts on the Bill."

"Who, may I ask?"

"Senator Britt Clayton and Senator Murphy Clark."

"Interesting, I thought I had won over both of their votes. What's up with them?"

"Funding, what else?"

"Well, the money is there. They need to work on the appropriations. I can't believe anyone wouldn't want to help the children of this state, and I suspect other states and even countries. This country is going down the tubes."

"Now, Cynthia. You know I'll do everything I can. I need you in here to whip them into shape."

"I'll see you in your office at ten sharp tomorrow morning. The vote isn't until the afternoon. I'll work them over well," said Cynthia.

chapter

4

Jeffrey was developing a plan. His 'business partner' was sent an encrypted message. They were to meet tonight and discuss it at his house. His wife was visiting her parents, who lived out of town, so it would be a safe place for them to have a private and discreet discussion.

He loved his wife, but since they married, he found that her time away helped them both. She was high maintenance; however, she was a very beautiful woman; she was also bright and would be able to decipher anything she overheard. That was why he kept most of his business at the office. He knew his occasional dalliances were not something she would approve of, so he had to be careful.

Despite having a vast wardrobe, Stella spent most of her time shopping. She was constantly redecorating the house, even though it was beautifully decorated. They rarely had company, except for her family. She had two sisters who lived out of state, so they seldom visited. Her parents would pop in occasionally, usually on the way to another destination. She had a nightly skin care regimen that took almost an hour. After all, she was an heir to one of the largest skincare companies in the world. She received her products for free, so there was no complaint there. Many women, he knew, spent thousands per year on the same thing Stella used.

Their honeymoon was a European cruise, the best he could afford then. His career at a hedge fund company was quite lucrative, and he had been able to afford the better things in life. They married in June of 2007, and there were rumors of problems in the market then. It went downhill from there. He had made several million, but he found out on their cruise how his wife liked to spend lavishly.

He expected the sex would continue to be exceptional after they married as it was before, but he was in for a surprise. Before they wed, they had sex regularly, and she gave an Oscar-worthy performance. How was he to know that she hated having intercourse? She allowed him his due, but that was all. She didn't perform the way she had before the nuptials. No oral sex and no shower sex; it deflated his ego. He had never displeased a woman before, so he wasn't expecting Stella to become so turned off by his advances. She wanted to shop and eat and lie on the deck. He found himself in the casinos more, looking for another partner.

He got lucky one afternoon when he had an encounter with one of the casino workers. She was a German girl working for the summer between her junior and senior years at Cambridge. He could see that she noticed him looking at her often, especially her low-cut tee shirt. He guessed the casino requested they wear skimpy clothes while working to keep the customers happy. One afternoon, she slipped him her room number, which he knew had to be on the bottom deck. The staff generally didn't have nice quarters; they were about the size of a broom closet. She put a time, which was thirty minutes later.

He looked for Stella and found her on the sun deck, reading a book and conversing with the woman beside her. He kissed her on the cheek and told her he would nap in the room. She said, "Okay," and waved him off. He knew he was in the clear. Thirty minutes later, he was in Gretchen's tiny room, where their dalliance had to be quick and quiet. However, it was the best sex he had had in weeks, not since he was with Katarina before he got married.

He was only twelve when he had his first sexual encounter with one of the housekeepers. She taught him how to satisfy a woman. When he went to college, he became popular with the girls in no time. He had multiple girlfriends, which he would get mixed up often, but they never seemed to mind as long as he was willing to pleasure them. When he realized they were as oversexed as he was, he quit worrying about mixing them up.

He enjoyed daydreaming and remembering these escapades but was snapped back to reality when the doorbell rang. "So good of you to come," said Jeffrey as he allowed Britt into the entry hall.

"No problem, your message sounded urgent."

"It's not urgent, but an idea I wanted to discuss with you, and if you approve, I will put it in motion. We have been asked to get younger girls for Cobbler. He was being pressured to provide underage girls for the sickos he took on his cruises. My words, not his. I am leery of trying to lure younger girls. Do you think we could kidnap a couple to satisfy them, at least for a little while?"

"Kidnap?"

"I know, it's a felony. If we are caught, it is the penitentiary. But we won't get caught. I have been on the dark web, and there are kidnapping tips and tricks. It's not terribly hard. Evil, yes. But if we only do it a couple of times, then go back to picking up pros, it will blow over."

"I don't know," said his partner, Britt.

"I've got a guy I believe will take care of it. He has done other things rather unsavory for me, so this would be a walk in the park for him."

"I don't know, Jeffrey, let me sleep on it," said Britt.

"Okay, but don't take too long."

"I won't. How about we go out for a steak?"

"I've made other plans, sorry. The wife's out of town, and I have a little treat coming over tonight for midnight dessert."

"You devil you. I wish I had the nerve to try, but I have to say, I am happy where I live. My wife makes sure of it."

"You are a lucky man," said Jeffrey as he rose to walk Britt to the door.

"I will call you when I have made up my mind. It is a big lift, I mean severe," said Britt.

Jeffrey called his contact, who was on his yacht. He used a SAT phone, so he was always available. He knew the man loved to listen to Sinatra music because he could hear it playing in the background, so he wondered if his real name was Frank.

"Yes, do you have any news for me?" asked the man.

"It is probable, but I need a few days."

"No worries, take your time, but make sure it is worth our wait," he chuckled at his stupid joke.

Jeffrey was itching to get things taken care of now. He was glad his wife was out so he could have recreational fun and time to think. The doorbell rang, which meant Veronica had arrived. He loved it when his wife was out of town. If only she would go more often. Veronica was one of his college girlfriends. She married well and had two teenage daughters, whom she chose to send to boarding school. Her husband, whom she loved very much, died suddenly three years ago while bicycling. He had a brain aneurysm.

"At least he didn't suffer," she told Jeffrey when they began their affair.

It started after he and Stella were married, at a wedding for one of Stella's sisters. It happened innocently as he walked toward the bar during the reception, and she was coming out of the restroom. She was there attending a different function. When they saw each other, fireworks ignited, and he couldn't have been more pleased to see her again. After they talked for a few minutes, she joined him in the bar. He knew Stella was safely tucked away talking with her sorority sisters, so he didn't think he would be noticed being gone for so long. To be sure, he walked back in and whispered in Stella's ear that he had run into an old friend in the bar, and they were having a drink. He didn't indicate that it was an old friend he had pleasured many times in college.

Stella waved him off, setting him free. He returned to the bar and suggested they take a walk outside. Veronica agreed, and they ended up in the backseat of Jeffrey's Mercedes. Their relationship continued and grew into a full-blown affair. She enjoyed seeing him whenever he was available, and no strings were attached. She was well off and had no desire to remarry.

She told Jeffrey, "I want to raise my beautiful twins and have many grandchildren."

chapter 5

Jeffrey was in his office reading the current news from Raleigh. He was on the political page reading about the new Bill. The legislature was almost through its session but still had a few Bills to settle before they would call a recess and go home. The one that most concerned him was Bill 23 ST 8003. He had already heard that Mrs. Cynthia Curtis had been to the State House, and she was the most prominent lobbyist for Human Trafficking in the state. The bill passed the House and was now about to be voted on in the Senate. He knew if it passed, the governor would sign it into law. It would affect his side business, possibly killing it altogether because it would keep him from recruiting younger girls. *If it wasn't one thing, it was another,* thought Jeffrey.

He used his burner phone to call his partner. "Have you made up your mind yet? I see the Bill will be voted on soon and probably pass," asked Jeffrey.

"I have, and if you have worked it out, we can try this once and see how it goes, but it will get more difficult in the future. I don't want to take another chance. I may have to bow out if it continues."

"Do you think the Bill could fail in the Senate?"

"It will pass. There are too many careers depending on it. It is a political hot potato."

"Okay, I agree, one and done. Hopefully, it will get Cobbler off our backs. Truth be told, he didn't sound very keen on it anyway. It takes a sick man to want to have sex with a child, in my opinion."

Jeffrey called his man to give him the green light. "We are ready to proceed. Please be careful. You said that you may have one picked out already?"

"Yes, I do. She will be easy pickings. I have followed her for a while; she is young and wild. Having sex with her dates. Can you imagine?"

Jeffrey chuckled. "Do you have a timeline in mind?"

"I am working with Walter. We are readying a house on one of your properties. It is off Senior Road, the one you plan to put up for sale. There's a basement we were going to soundproof. Does that sound good? Will you have transport when necessary?"

"Yes, she will be moved to an interim location, then another, before she is ready for the final transport. I am working with others; you will hear when it is ready to execute. From my research, it is best to keep them moving so fewer eyes will be on the subject at any time. Yes, that property's perfect. Walter must have told you about it. He has a credit card he can use to purchase the materials. Tell him it is okay, but to save the receipt for me. Just be smart, which I know you will. You haven't let me down before. Contact me on the phone number I last gave you when it happens. I'll keep it on me."

"Okay, boss. Later," he hung up.

Jeffrey hoped Vinnie was up to this task. He had helped him out before with sensitive issues that came up. The last big one was Jeffrey's mistake on a trip to Las Vegas. He stayed at Caesars but liked to go to the seedier strip clubs in the evening. One evening, he was in a club, and there was the most beautiful girl he had ever seen. She gave him a lap dance, which led to another, and he slipped his card into a hundred-dollar bill and put it in her G-string. He noted she had small breasts, but the rest of the package was perfect.

He tucked it in so management would not see it on their cameras. He left and returned to the hotel, hoping she would call. Around eleven, he was just about to order a porn flick when his cell phone rang, and it was her. She told him she was getting off work soon and wondered if he wanted to see her. He gave her his room number, and she arrived a little after midnight. She was more beautiful than he had noticed in the dark strip club. She had lovely auburn hair, which she wore very long, almost to her waist. She had it up in a ponytail during her shift, which made her even sexier. Her skin was pale, and she had big brown eyes.

He asked her why she was stripping, and she told him she tried Hollywood, but when that didn't work out, she was at a loss for what to do. She had a friend from back home in West Virginia with whom she kept in regular contact. Her friend had started stripping in Las Vegas, and she invited her to come and stay with her; she agreed and hoped she could get a job at the same place she worked. She arrived the next day, applied where her friend worked, and got the job. She had been asked to remove her top and bra when she tried out for a part in a movie, but other than that, she had never done anything like it before.

"Do you ever do escort services?" asked Jeffrey. "Not until now," she replied.

"Are you on birth control?"

"Yes, I am on the pill."

Jeffrey reached out and pulled her close. He proceeded to unbutton her blouse and saw she had a lovely bustline with a pushup bra. He felt her breasts through the bra, which ignited purrs from her; they were small, as he noted at the club, but were high and perky. She reached up and kissed him on the lips, and he put his right hand on her bra clasp, and before she knew it, she had her shirt and bra off. He watched as she removed her jeans and underwear and stood before him. He removed his shirt and pants. Jeffrey pulled a condom from the bedside table because he didn't want to take any chances. There's also the STD concern, so he always made sure he had plenty on hand.

They spent the next two days in his room enjoying each other's body and ordered room service between their sexual acts. He couldn't get enough of her. When it was time for him to leave, he gave her $5,000 in cash. He figured he would have lost it in the casino, so why not? He promised to get in touch the next time he was in town.

About two months later, he received a call from her, and she said she was pregnant and it was his. "How do you know?" Jeffrey was incredulous. He knew she must have had multiple sex partners since then, and he knew he used a condom each time they had intercourse.

"I just know. I haven't had sex since we were together; I'll do a DNA test if you want me to."

He told her that wouldn't be necessary and that he would be back in touch. Instead, he called Vinnie and purchased him a plane ticket to 'take care of the problem.' He hadn't heard from the young lady since, and Vinnie never told him how he handled it.

Jeffrey knew that wealthy men were targets for blackmail. He took a chance, but it wasn't the first time. It happened when he was in college, and a girl did get pregnant. He got careless one day. He was in class; he could not even remember which one, but he had his eye on this girl in front of him. She had a pair of shorts on and had the longest and shapeliest legs he had ever seen.

After class, he 'accidentally' knocked one of his books off his table and into her back. She turned around, annoyed at first, but he apologized profusely and immediately asked her to go to the coffee shop if she had time so he could buy her a cup of coffee. She agreed when she saw how sincere he seemed. After an hour of coffee and talking, he walked her to her dorm, and she invited him in. What he didn't know at the time was that she knew of his reputation, and she wanted him in her dorm room for sex.

As soon as they were alone, she unbuttoned her shorts and unzipped her pants so he could see she had no underwear. She came onto him, and before he knew it, he was lying on his back in her bed. They were completely naked, and she was on top of him. He could tell this wasn't her first rodeo. She had large, full breasts to go with her long, lovely legs. This was one time he had not used a condom because he didn't have any on him. He had run out and was lax about restocking. She had assured him she was on the pill. They had sex for the rest of the afternoon and night. He left at dawn to get back in time for a shower and prepare for another class.

They met at least twice a week for the next four weeks for pure, unadulterated sex. She expected nothing else from him, and he always wore a condom. She didn't have a roommate, so they were not in danger of getting caught. She was in a co-ed dorm, and sex was very much part of the scene. After the semester was over, their meet-ups waned. He wasn't sure why, but she always had an excuse.

About four weeks later, she called him and told him she was pregnant and it had to be his. She apologized and said she was definitely on the pill, but it had to be that one time they had multiple intercourse without protection. He talked her into getting an abortion because they were in no way compatible as a couple, and neither wanted to get married. She agreed, and he paid for it. He even went with her to the clinic and took her back to her friend's apartment, where she stayed for a few days. He never saw or heard from her again.

chapter

6

Angela watched the clock, hoping her mother would get home soon so she and Brent could hang out tonight. She played with her brother all afternoon and wanted to take a shower. She asked Andy to watch the movie she found on the Disney Channel while she cleaned up and showered. He promised her he would. His little eyelids looked droopy, so she expected he would be asleep soon. He climbed up on the sofa with a pillow, and it wasn't long before he quieted down.

Andy was her half-brother. His father, Ken Harper, married her mother when she was only ten years old, and her mom had Andy not too long after that. Now that she was older, she understood better why they married in such a hurry. Her father left when her mom became pregnant with her. She was still in high school, and he didn't want to get accused of statutory rape. Angela never met him. She stayed with her grandmother when her mother worked. Her grandmother had done the best she could, but she had never finished high school and wasn't what she would now consider to be a nurturing type. Her mother had made remarks in the past about her upbringing, but since her grandmother passed away at least five years ago before her mother married Ken, they rarely spoke of her. Ken was the only father figure she ever had, but the marriage didn't work out, and they divorced about two years ago. Ken faithfully pays his child support. He's a well-employed long-haul truck driver. He loved Andy, and she thought he still loved her, too. He would send extra gifts to them at Christmas, and he still remembered her birthday. He was a great guy, and she wished they were still married.

Angela finished cleaning up the kitchen. She made spaghetti sauce the way her grandmother used to the few times she would cook. She left it on the stove but turned the power off. She went into their only bathroom, showered, and washed her hair. Afterward, she got out her electric razor and shaved her legs. She put lotion on and proceeded to dry her beautiful silky blonde hair. She rarely wore makeup but decided to add some eye makeup and lipstick.

She found her clean white shorts and a new sleeveless top that she got when she and her mom went on a shopping trip just before school let out. It was one of the rare times they were able to go alone. Ken had come into town and wanted to spend time with Andy. He took him to a movie and out to eat. Due to his trucking schedule, Andy didn't see him often, but he enjoyed every visit. Ken made sure to make him feel special. Her mom mentioned that Ken might be remarrying, but it had been a while since she said that, and she hoped he had changed his mind. She would hate for Andy to be neglected in any way.

She quietly walked into the living room, and as expected, she found Andy asleep on the sofa. At about that time, she heard the door being unlocked, so she knew her mother was home. She smiled at her mom and said, "Did you have a good day?"

Her mother grunted but smiled and said, "It was busy but not bad. What did y'all do all day? I got the message about the milk." She held up a gallon for Angela to see.

Angela told her about their day and that she had made spaghetti sauce on the stove.

"May I go out tonight with Brent, please?" asked Angela.

"Yes, that would be fine. I see Andy is asleep. Do you want to eat here, or are y'all planning on going somewhere?"

"I think we will go to the burger place in town called Hwy 55." It was one of the newest places in their small town.

"Okay, then I'll make the pasta, and if Andy wakes up, he can eat, but if not, he may be famished in the morning," she laughed.

"I agree, but I will take care of him in the morning. I promise to be in by midnight, okay?" asked Angela.

"Sure."

Angela texted Brent: *It's a go; come and get me as soon as possible before she changes her mind.* She added a question mark emoji.

Brent was from what Angela considered to be a 'normal' family. He had a mother and father in the home. He also had two sisters; one was older and in her first year at NC State, and the other was three years younger than Brent and was giving her parents a hard time. She knew he worried about Lisa and tried to help his parents by watching after her.

She was a wild child who sneaked out with boyfriends she was too young to have; she constantly defied anything her parents forbade.

Brent told her a while back that he figured out his parents had to get married because his mother was pregnant with his older sister. He said he was looking at their wedding album one day, and that's when he figured out their wedding date and his sister's birthday seven months later; he put two and two together and knew then why they got married when they did. But fortunately for him, they were made for each other and would have married eventually.

His father started his own business. He was an excavator and gravel supplier. He worked in the summers during high school for a company in South Carolina and learned the trade. He loved being outside and being a part of the building industry. Williams Brothers was the name of the company. Initially, it was just him, and the business was named Williams Gravel and Excavation, but he had more business than he could handle. Eventually, his brother, Daniel, partnered with him, turning the company into a tri-county million-dollar-a-year business. His wife Michelle went to the community college and took accounting, so she managed the books and ran the office. They hoped Brent would eventually take over the day-to-day grind so they would have some retirement time, but that was way in the future. Brent planned to attend NC State and hoped to qualify for a football scholarship.

"Bye, Mom. Brent is here," Angela called to her mom. Andy slept right through the commotion. Brenda stuck her head out of the kitchen and greeted Brent.

"Y'all be careful and have fun."

"Good to see you, Mrs. Harper. We'll be careful; you can count on it," said Brent.

They no sooner got in the car than Brent leaned over, put his hand on her thigh, and kissed her.

"I'm glad to see you, too," said Angela, giggling.

"Are you hungry?" asked Brent.

"A little, can we try the new place, Hwy 55? I told my mom we would probably go there so she may ask me about it."

"We sure can." He cranked the truck and rolled out of her gravel driveway.

When they arrived at Hwy 55, they realized they were hungry. They each had burgers and shakes. Brent had fries, but Angela passed on them. She knew the shake had ruined her attempt at dieting, and the fries were a no-no.

Afterward, Brent drove out to a clearing at the top of a cliff they found a few weeks ago. It was small so that they would have privacy. Brent had no intention of going all the way with Angela. He respected her and felt one day they would get married. He wanted to get through college, and he didn't want to have any regrets about their future. He knew things could happen if his parents got married when they did. He loved his family and didn't want to disappoint them.

It was a dark night, and the stars were so bright. Angela loved looking at the stars and when the night was still. The moon was just a sliver in the dark sky. She grabbed the blanket from the backseat, and they lay on the grass in an open area. No one else was around. It was a warm evening early in June. She had been dating Brent since last year. Her mother liked him. "He comes from good stock," said her mom. She thought that because he was a Williams, and his father and uncle owned the largest company in Blaylock County, he was quite a catch for Angela.

She told Brent she needed to find a place to relieve herself, so she got up from their blanket, where they had just begun petting under the stars. She told him she would be right back, and she walked over toward the tree line and went a little deeper into the forest. It was a slight hill, but she found a good spot to do her business. As she was finishing, she heard voices at the bottom of the gulley. She quickly got her pants pulled up and zipped. She walked down just a little farther. These hills carried voices quite loudly, so it was hard to tell how far away the sounds were. But then, she heard a man's voice say, "I'm telling you, she would be very easy to capture and take with us. We must make up our minds soon."

A different voice said, "I know, but the timing and the place have to be right; if we get caught, there will be hell to pay. From the little I have read, the bidding that goes on for that age was incredible, and the longer they can bid on her, the better, so we are in a good location for a selection. I say go for it if you are almost ready. Call me tomorrow."

Then she heard the closing of car doors and two engines rev up. She thought one might be a truck, but the tree boughs were too thick, and she could only see car lights. She believes they were dark in color. She wasn't sure what she just heard meant. *Are they talking about kidnapping?* She wondered. They mentioned someone young, or the age was good; she wasn't sure. She knew that didn't sound good and wanted to get back up the hill and tell Brent. She turned and headed up the hill, but in her haste, she slipped on loose rocks and fell; not able to catch her fall, she rolled down the hill quite a bit and stopped when she crashed into a large boulder, which she hit her head on; she started to get up but then saw nothing but black.

She realized she must have passed out because she heard Brent calling her name and his cell phone light on her face. She was disoriented but thought she wasn't injured badly. He helped her up, saying, "I was worried about you and had difficulty finding you. Are you okay?"

She stood with his help and looked at him, dazed, and said, "I'm okay, please take me home."

He walked her up the hill, and they got in his truck and drove to her house. It was past her curfew of twelve, but he hoped her mom wouldn't be upset, considering everything that had happened. When Mrs. Harper came to the door, she took one look at Angela and opened the screen to help Brent get her in the house and into bed. "I'm not sure, but she may have hit her head on something; she acted like she had passed out. It took me a while to find her."

"What do you mean find her?" Brenda asked Brent accusingly.

Brent didn't know what to say. He realized he hadn't thought through how to explain this to Mrs. Harper. At this point, he decided the best action was to tell her the truth. "We did go to get a bite to eat at Hwy 55 and hung out there with some of our friends for a while. It was getting late, but we wanted to be, er, alone, so we went to this little spot off of Hwy 408 and were sitting on the back of my truck gate looking up at the stars. Angela's a stargazer."

He was not sure Mrs. Harper was buying this last part but continued, "Angela told me she needed to go to the bathroom, so she walked over to a hidden area and walked down a little way, and after she did her business, she was coming back up to the truck but slipped and rolled down the hill. I couldn't see her because it was so dark out there, but I finally located her, and she was coming around; it was probably no more than fifteen minutes. I hope you're not mad."

"I'm not mad, Brent. I appreciate that you did the right thing and brought her straight home. You might just come up with a better story the next time," then she winked at him.

"Yes, ma'am," Brent said.

"I'll stay in her room and keep an eye on her, and I'll take her to the hospital in the morning if she has any serious symptoms. I read somewhere that it's best to keep them awake, but I don't think that will work. If she starts vomiting, I'll take her to the hospital, but I think we'll be all right. Thank you for taking such good care of her, Brent." He knew he needed to go now and let them rest, but he was still worried about her.

When Brent arrived home, he could see that his dad's light in his study was on, which meant he was still up. He stuck his head in the door and told him he was home safe and sound. Then he proceeded to tell him about Angela's fall. He left out why they were in the open on a blanket. His dad, who liked Angela, was smart enough to read between the lines. "I'm afraid she may have a concussion, but Mrs. Harper wanted to wait until the morning to take her to the hospital if need be."

"She will watch her, don't worry about it. She should be okay if she could get into your truck and walk up to her house. Why don't you call first thing in the morning to make sure? I can see that you are worried."

"Okay, Dad. I'll see you in the morning. Is Lisa home?"

"No, spending the night with a girlfriend." Brent wondered.

chapter 7

Lisa Williams, Brent's younger sister, was hitting her peak of puberty. Her parents had the most trouble with her of all three of their children. For one thing, she was tall and had a beautiful figure for her age. She had long blond hair and blue eyes. She went from being a tomboy to being crazy about boys almost overnight. Her mother grounded her for sneaking out, driving with a sixteen-year-old driver, and wearing eye makeup to school. She had been a challenge.

Tonight, she planned a sleepover with her best friend, Tiffany Armano. At least, that was what she told her mother. Her mother will check with Mrs. Armano and find out if they plan to have Lisa over. Mrs. Armano will confirm, and later in the evening, after they go to bed, Lisa tends to sneak out of their house to go off with her latest boyfriend, Stewart Mankiewicz. She hoped to return before anyone got up.

When she was only twelve years old, Lisa went to the school nurse and told her she thought she should get on birth control. It was no problem, and no questions were asked. She was given a year's supply of pills. Her mother still didn't know she was taking them. Just in case the school nurse won't give them to her again, she planned to plead with her mother this summer, telling her all the girls took them for cramps from heavy periods. She thinks her mother will be okay with it, but it could be another story if she asked her father. She would have to come up with another plan. She had already lost her virginity, so she justified being on the pill because she was doing them a favor by not getting pregnant. If they only knew how often she already had sex. She wasn't the only one; she knew at least a dozen girls her age who had already gone all the way with their boyfriends. The peer pressure was strong to do so.

Her school was public and considered up-scale. Most of the Juniors were gifted cars when they turned sixteen. Stewart got his license a month ago, and his father bought him a used Jeep Bronco for his birthday. That car was where she planned to have her fun tonight.

Her brother wouldn't approve of her having sex either. He had a girlfriend, a poor girl named Angela. She felt sorry for Angela because she knew she had a single mom, and they had little to no money. They lived in a double-wide off of a gravel road on the opposite side of town. Angela didn't seem to judge her and stayed out of her way. She wondered at times if Brent and Angela had sex yet. She thought not because Brent wouldn't want to do anything to upset his chances of going to NC State. Her older sister was there now and was probably having the time of her life. She was the brainiac of the family, so she would also be keeping up with her studies. She was talking about attending medical school, and Lisa had no doubt she was smart enough to be accepted.

It was time for her mother to get home, so she went to get her bag ready so she could get to Tiffany's as soon as possible. She was sitting out on the front porch when her mother drove up. She got in the car and said, "Hi, mom. Did you have a good day?"

"Yes, did you get your chores done?

"I did and even did my laundry."

"Thank you. I appreciate that very much."

When they arrived at Tiffany's house, her mom walked her to the door, and Mrs. Armano came out on the porch. "Hi, Lisa. How are you doing, Michelle?"

"I'm doing great. I appreciate you inviting her over for a night. She needed to get out of the house. I know they get bored during the summer, especially when the parents work, like me," she chuckled.

"No worries. What time do you want to pick her up tomorrow? We're not going anywhere, so anytime is good."

"Lisa, why don't you call or text tomorrow when you are ready to be picked up? But don't stay too late and wear out your welcome," Michelle said.

"Sure, mom. I'll do that." Michelle kissed her daughter's cheek and then left to drive home. It's been a long week, and she couldn't wait for a bubble bath.

Tiffany and Lisa spent the evening talking about who they liked and about their sexual encounters. Tiffany told her she was in between seeing anyone. She had broken up with Barry Smith just before school was out. Barry played sports, particularly baseball, and he would be on a travel team all summer and wouldn't be around much. Tiffany didn't like that, so they mutually agreed they would call it quits and see what happened when school started back. She told Lisa she liked him and hoped they would renew seeing each other. "I'm not going to wait for him, though. If someone else comes along, I would be willing to date them. It's hard to meet anyone during the summer, though."

After they were sure Tiffany's parents were asleep, Tiffany led Lisa downstairs, and she went out the back door. It was extremely dark, with barely any light from the quarter moon. She walked to the end of the driveway, using her cell phone for light, where Stewart picked her up. She had her tightest and shortest shorts on with a crop top. Since she developed early, she had a full bosom, which she showed off well with a pushup bra that Tiffany loaned her.

When she got in the passenger seat, Stewart growled and seemed pleased. "Hurry up, let's get out of here before they see us," she told him.

They drove to the lookout bluff where the older teenagers hang out. Only two cars were there, but it was already after midnight. Most curfews were eleven. She wasn't supposed to be dating, so she hadn't technically been given a curfew. Stewart was all over her after he turned the ignition off. She knew she had the reputation of being 'easy,' which was well deserved. This would be their first night going all the way. She knew Stewart wasn't a novice. She had heard other girls talk about having sex with him. For some odd reason, Lisa thought having sex with other girl's boyfriends was a sport. She considered it quite an accomplishment. She sometimes wondered what made her feel that way. Her parents didn't like that she was on social media. They would be shocked if they only knew how it influenced virtually every facet of her life. They had no idea she was the school slut and was proud of it. Well, maybe Brent knows by now. He would give her odd looks now and then. She hoped she wouldn't get pregnant because that would complicate her life big time, not to mention the upset her family would endure.

She crawled in the backseat and removed her jean shorts. Her bikini panties and bra were all she had left on. Stewart removed his pants and left his t-shirt in place. He pulled out a condom from his wallet. After some petting, they were both aroused, and he helped her remove her bra and panties; afterward, it took them both a few minutes to catch their breath. Stewart had opened the front windows. About the time they were redressed, they heard a car crank its engine. It backed up and shined its lights into their car. Out of courtesy, the occupants didn't do that to each other. They ducked down as low as possible but were afraid it may have been too late.

"That was weird," said Stewart.

"Yes, it was," exclaimed Lisa. They just hoped it wasn't a cop or someone's parents checking out the place. It was a car neither of them recognized.

Stewart dropped her off about a half hour later, and she sneaked back into the Armanos' house. She decided not to tell Tiffany that night because she didn't want to upset her. She would wait until tomorrow to tell her. The car lights rattled her, and she reluctantly decided this would be her last time sneaking out for a while.

chapter

8

Vinnie had seen enough to know that the blond girl in the jeep would be the one to snatch. She was obviously hypersexual. He had his eye on her for a while and figured out she was a favorite of the young men. He hung out at the local burger joint for the last week, hoping to find a prospect for Mr. Edwards. He watched and listened.

It didn't take too long for him to hear a couple of guys in a booth behind him talking about how a girl named Lisa 'put out.' They used foul language between them. One of the guys mentioned he was getting a jeep for his birthday, so he would have a vehicle to take the girls out and have fun. Vinnie knew the younger generation X, or whatever they called themselves, used sexual escapades as recreation. When he was in school, there were a few girls that all the boys, especially the football team, would go to when they had sexual tension. Someone like him couldn't get to first base with those girls. He was lucky to have one of them look at him sideways.

These days, though, according to his nephews, they just had to ask a girl out and take her to a movie; the next thing they knew, they were in the back seat going at it. His nephews confided in him, but he had to promise not to tell their mother.

He learned about the 'Lover's Lane' by accident. He followed a couple from the burger joint, and they went straight there. He parked and waited. It took a while, but finally, he saw a jeep pull up. He noticed the front windows get cracked, a sure sign. The next thing he knew, he heard moaning and the steam in the back windows. Jeeps are small, and heating them up doesn't take much. He knew who was in the car because of overhearing the stooge Stewart mentioned at the burger joint the night before that he expected to get some 'pussy' from Lisa, the slut, the next night. Vinnie had gotten her name clandestinely before by bumping into her at the mall and pretending she was someone else. She told him her name, and he apologized.

He cranked the car and shined the lights into the jeep, a little for fun and to give them something to chew on. His plan was perfect. He had the right girl. Now, his plan needed to be put into action. He was going to see Walter later tonight. The place had to be fixed up until they could get her transferred. He will get a message to the big guy ASAP.

Vinnie wasn't so far removed from Generation X. He had only been out of high school for ten years, barely graduating. His home life had been a train wreck with an out-of-work father and a mother who tried to keep them afloat, but she worked herself to the bone doing so. His dad had been a bum from what he had known of him.

He would come and go from their lives. Vinnie was the youngest of four. His two older sisters made it out as soon as they could get jobs after high school. His only brother managed to earn a soccer scholarship to a small college in Virginia. He wasn't only talented but also intelligent. He was the success story of their family. His sisters married and had children but struggled to raise their kids and work. He was glad he was still single and had no desire to marry.

Sure, he enjoyed the company of the opposite sex, but it was sporadic. His work life was irregular. He hadn't been able to hold a job due to his ADHD. It was diagnosed late and was one reason he did so poorly in school. He was lucky to meet Mr. Edwards. It was just by chance. He was riding the subway in NYC one day, and a well-dressed gentleman got on at the Midtown stop and sat across from him. He had nowhere to go and was riding the subway to pass the time. He had a chance to work at the Garden that night and was waiting for a call. He sometimes helped out with one of the concessions.

While the train was moving, a Hispanic man walked up to the man across from him, pulled a gun, and attempted to rob him. He saw there was no one nearby, so he quickly grabbed the man from behind and put him in a chokehold. They fell to the floor, at which time the gun slipped from the man's hand and slid to the other end of the train. The perp was too strung out to defend himself, so he gave it up almost immediately. Vinnie kept him down until the next stop. The well-dressed man got up calmly and hailed security.

Security was there quickly and took the man in custody, gun included. They got the names of the only two witnesses and asked them to be available to give statements. He and the man gave their accounts immediately to the police officer in charge.

Afterward, the man gave him his card and said, "Call me."

He called him later that night, and they met the next day. He had been his go-to person ever since. It was a win/win for Vinnie and Mr. Edwards. However, it did require a move to North Carolina, a state he had never even visited.

Vinnie knew he had hit the jackpot. He had no prospects, wasn't a college candidate, and had no other skills. He was good with people and could size them up pretty quickly. If that were a talent, he would use it to the fullest.

Jeffrey Edwards had plenty of work for him. His first assignment was to fly to Vegas and handle the 'problem' Jeffrey Edwards had on his hands. The girl was gorgeous, and he wished to take her out and have fun with her. But he was sent for one reason, and that was to get her to either fess up if she was not pregnant or to convince her to get an abortion. After identifying her from Jeffrey's description, he confronted her as she left the strip club; she denied knowing what he was talking about. Vinnie convinced her to go for a cup of coffee.

After talking it through, she admitted to him that she wasn't pregnant and assured him she would not contact Jeffrey again. She told him she realized it was wrong but knew he was rich and decided to try a scam. "Sometimes, when you are desperate, you do stupid things, and this was one of them," she told him.

They spent two hours together just spilling their guts, and after they were through, he hailed a cab and took her home. He gave her a check for $1,000, which Jeffrey authorized him to do if she dropped it. She was stunned and started crying. He left her and headed to the airport. Fait Accompli.

chapter

9

Lisa and her friends had a ritual every Friday during the summer. They would take their allowance money, which was significant, and go to the local mall. Their parents didn't mind since there wasn't much else to do for young girls. They had fun trying on clothes they knew they would never buy, much less wear. They usually got some jewelry at Claire's, so they could afford a pretzel or Gyros at the food court. Today, there were six of them converging on the mall. Security was tighter on Fridays and weekends because of shoplifters. The big city problems had hit even small-town malls.

Sydney's brother Sly had offered to take them today. They all crunched in his silver Jeep and played the stereo as loud as they wanted. Post Malone was their favorite.

That afternoon proved to be so much fun, as usual. They giggled and mocked each other as they tried on outfits. They loved to make the store clerks mad to the point that they gave them stern, uncomfortable stares, hoping they would move on. After several hours and getting somewhat tired of modeling clothes, they went to the food court. It was already four o'clock, and Sly was to pick them up at five.

"Order me a large pretzel and medium root beer. I'll be right back.

I have to go to the bathroom," Lisa told her friend, Tiffany. Then added, "Please watch my purse, too." She proceeded to the bathroom, which was across from Chick-fil-A. The bathroom appeared empty except for a little old lady trying to go through her small purse. When Lisa entered the stall, she felt the door shoved into her as she went to lock it.

She started to scream, but before she could, she felt an injection in her upper arm and passed out, falling backward. Her attacker quickly dressed her in a wig, hat, and skirt that he was able to slip up her long legs somehow. She was so limp that she was easy to maneuver. He wrapped a shawl around her shoulders, hiding her skimpy top and shorts. He then stood her up and slipped out of the bathroom, partially dragging her along. The hat concealed most of her face. Her friends were at a table quite a distance away and were all engrossed in looking at their phones. *That was the beauty of Americans; they only think of them-selves and hardly look up from their cell phones*, thought Walter. Vinnie was just outside the mall door with the car running.

Walter opened the back door and placed Lisa inside. She fell over on the seat, and he saw she was still passed out. She was turned on her side, which was good in case she vomited. Walter hopped in the front seat, undressing quickly from his disguise.

"It was so easy. I got lucky because the bathroom was virtually empty. One person came in while I was dressing her, but they remained in the stall while I straightened her up and walked her out. The bathrooms were so convenient to the door. Do you think we should contact mall security and suggest a flaw in the design? Hey, we could start being consultants. I heard it was quite lucrative," he chuckled at his joke. But it did make sense, so he was considering it. The problem was that he knew he didn't have the brains it would take to put such a proposition together.

"We got lucky that she was the only one to go to the bathroom. I would have called it off otherwise."

They were easing out of the mall at a reasonable speed so as not to cause anyone to notice them. Vinnie knew the police would be watching the videotapes any time now. He didn't want to give them any reason to notice them. Two lights away was the expressway, so he eased into the lane to turn going south. Once on, he knew they were safe.

"I doubt those airhead friends will miss her for another thirty minutes. I followed them all day, and it couldn't have been more boring. She left her purse on the table, so I presumed her cell was in it. To be sure, I felt her up and didn't feel a phone," said Walter.

Lisa started stirring in the back seat. Walter reached into his pocket and got out the other needle. He leaned over the console so he could reach her and stuck her in her thigh, which was close and showing so well. She quit moving again, but he noticed drool coming out of her mouth, so he reached back, took a Kleenex out of his pocket, and wiped her mouth.

Vinnie called Jeffrey. "Yes?"

"It is done," said Vinnie.

"Okay, take her where you planned. Call me when she's settled in. I'm monitoring the news now."

They had prepared a place in the base of a house Jeffrey owned. They soundproofed one of the rooms in the basement. Jeffrey thought it was a wise investment he could afford; he wasn't sure if he would remove the soundproofing or leave it. A potential home buyer would probably think it was a kid playing the drums and driving his parents up the wall. Hopefully, they wouldn't suspect anything nefarious.

When it was over, they could easily remove and discard the material if they wanted it done. The beauty of it was that it was on a dead-end street, and there were no houses close to it. A barn was in the back, so any extra cars could be hidden.

Walter monitored her to ensure she didn't wake up when they pulled into the driveway. Unfortunately, there was no garage, so they had to be careful when they got her out and carried her inside the side door. To be sure, Walter crawled in the backseat and used flex cuffs on her ankles and wrists. Then he put a scarf in her mouth and tied it behind her head. He admired her long, curvy legs. She had fair skin with lovely, long blond air. He thought she was beautiful, but his appetite wasn't for underage girls, no matter what.

Vinnie got her under the arms, and as he pulled her out, Walter grabbed her ankles. He had already opened the door, so nothing obstructed the way to the basement. Once down there, Vinnie checked the cameras and brought her some bottled water for when she woke up. He adjusted the temperature to 73 degrees. He thought it was chilly down there at 70. They kept the overhead fluorescent lights on and laid her on the single bed. She had a pillow, blanket, and sheets, so she should be comfortable. They aimed to please.

Lisa slept for the next four hours. Vinnie monitored her on his laptop, and Walter watched a baseball game on their set-up TV. So far, there hadn't been anything on the news. They had been checking their phones and waiting. Jeffrey should call if anything pops up. They had stocked food, but mostly frozen meals. They had milk, cereal, fruit, and a few snacks. As she started waking up, they could see on the monitor that all hell was about to break loose. Her feet were untied, but her wrists were still bound. They removed the scarf as soon as they put her on the bed.

Vinnie said, "Here we go, get ready." He jumped up and grabbed the flex cuffs in case. Walter followed him down the stairs. She was screaming at the top of her lungs, and her profanity embarrassed even them.

"Hey, hey," said Vinnie. "You want to calm down now. No one can hear you. You can see the room is soundproof. You are only going to get a sore throat."

"Why am I here?" screamed Lisa.

"That, I can't tell you right now, but it will be evident soon enough."

"If it is money you want, just contact my father. He will give you anything you want."

"Sorry, but we are just the messengers." Walter pulled out another syringe and approached her.

"No, please not again, don't knock me out," begged Lisa.

"It is for your own good," Walter said, injecting her in her thigh, which was the most accessible place.

chapter

10

The Sheriff of Blaylock County was pulling up to the soccer field to meet his son and watch his game when he got a call from the deputy on duty. He took the call, and what he heard piqued his interest quickly. "What did you say, Turner?"

Turner repeated, "There's been a missing person report filed on Lisa Williams."

Kellum asked, "Who?"

"Lisa is the youngest daughter of Trent and Michelle Williams, you know, Williams Brothers."

"Oh my God, really? She couldn't just be off with a friend?"

"It doesn't appear so. Her girlfriends called her parents. You need to get over here."

"On my way. Please initiate the Amber Alert before I arrive. Is Todd there? Perhaps he could do it."

"Yes, sir. I will start it. Todd can help. We don't have plates yet, and we are not sure if we will. Maybe we should hold out until we know the make of the car."

"Yes, probably. Tell Todd we will call him as soon as we get to the mall and get more information."

He told his son his mother would pick him up, and he was sorry he couldn't stay. His son was easygoing, and he understood. His daughter Beth was another story. She was going through the worst part of puberty and was hormonal and irrational. Shannon promised him it would pass, hopefully before they were both gray.

On the way, he called Shannon and explained what was going on. "I'll be late for sure. Don't wait up. Kellum knows you will be picking him up," he told her.

When he arrived at the station, several people, including the ubiquitous news media, were already there. They could be annoying, but he understood they also had a job to do. This was a big enough story that they wanted every tiny tidbit of information they could garner.

He was greeted by Deputy Turner McCall, who had so much to tell him he could hardly get it out fast enough. "Okay, hold on, Turner, you are going way too fast for me to comprehend. Please go slow and tell me what you know."

"Lisa and five of her friends were dropped off by one of the girl's brothers," he consulted his notes. "Sly is the name I have. They had gone to the food court at around four, and Lisa told Tiffany, her best friend, to get her a giant pretzel and root beer and that she would be right back because she needed to go to the bathroom. She left her purse, including her phone, with Tiffany.

"The next thing they knew, it was half an hour later, and she hadn't returned. They all ran into the bathroom but didn't see her. They started screaming her name, and security ran up. They immediately closed the entrances, wouldn't let anyone out, and called the police."

"Okay, let's get to the mall. We'll drive separately. Have the parents been notified?"

"Yes, her friends called her mother first. They should be there when we arrive."

Kellum knew this would be bad. They haven't had a kidnapping for as long as he can remember. A thirteen-year-old girl? His mind goes to one place. Sex Trafficking. He just returned a few months ago from a seminar in Chicago. It was incredibly well-organized and informative. He attended several classes and learned how the groomers locate their victims. Several people from a broad spectrum of law enforcement were there as speakers.

The southwestern states were getting hit the hardest, but that was due to the children coming across the border. He learned that the flesh peddlers, their term for these monsters, were also looking for young, white, prepubescent, or in puberty, girls and even boys. The information was so disturbing that he hated thinking about it, but he knew he must act on his training. Since the seminar, he had been processing everything and working on organizing a mandatory class for his deputies. Now this. They were going to be getting on-the-job training.

He pulled up at the entrance and saw the police and security officers. As he got out of the car, a man walked up and identified himself as the head of security for BEN Corporation, the mall's owner. Kellum introduced himself and asked where the video cameras were located.

"I have the videos ready to go, Chief Taylor. We have multiple vantage points."

Kellum followed the officer through the guarded doors into a makeshift command post. "Are the customers still in the mall, and have they been interviewed?" asked Kellum.

"Yes, sir, they have, and we have their contact information. Would it be okay to let them leave?"

"Make sure all their parking places are documented, including license plates. Let my deputies help you walk them out. They will have to be patient. Take the ones with small children first."

"Okay." He spoke in his wireless mike to his next in command and relayed what the chief had told him to do so they could clear out the mall.

Kellum was sitting in front of the computer, and another security person pulled up the video. They watched Lisa as she gave some money to a girl sitting at the table. Kellum made a mental note to find out which girl that was. She turned and walked toward the bathroom. Before they could go any further, he heard a man yelling, "I need to speak with someone; she's my daughter." Kellum looked up to see Trent and his wife coming toward him. He didn't want them to notice the video before he saw it, so he promptly stood up and walked toward them.

"Chief Taylor, please tell us what is going on," Trent said. Michelle held onto his arm, wide-eyed, and tried to hold back the tears.

Kellum did his best to calm them down but waved to the female security guard to help him. "I just got here, Trent and Michelle. I am so sorry, but I'm trying to find out everything I can now. The other girls are being interviewed. My deputies and the security personnel are letting some mall customers leave, but don't worry; they have their contact information. Please let me get as much information as possible, and then we will talk. Now, this nice young lady will take you to a place where you can sit down and get some water or coffee, whatever you want, and I will be right back with you as soon as I can." He nodded to the female officer, and she led them to another room so they would have some privacy.

Kellum saw the TV station out of Raleigh pulling up outside the door. They were setting up, hoping to get a shot for the evening news. He sat back down, looked at the officer, and said, "Now, show me."

They watched Lisa walk to the bathroom. The tape ran for just a few minutes. Another lady walked in there and had some shopping bags with her.

"Have you spoken with this woman?" asked Kellum to the video officer.

"I'm not sure, but I'm almost positive they have. I will check for you if you like."

"Let's watch the rest of the tape." A few more minutes go by, and then what appears to be a hunched-over woman comes out of the door, holding the hand of what looked like an elderly lady who could hardly walk. It looked like she was being dragged alongside her. "That's her!

Exclaimed Kellum. I know that is her. The kidnapper was in the bathroom, and all they had to do was put a wig on her, and no one knew the difference. Rewind it way before we saw Lisa the first time."

The officer did so, and that was when they saw the kidnapper go into the bathroom wearing a dress and wig and carrying a bag. "He was in there waiting on her or one of the girls she was with; that's how those bastards work."

"Are there any outside cameras on the door they exited and the parking lot?" implored Kellum.

The officer pulled up the outside tape and saw a dark sedan with four doors. Unfortunately, it was black and white but also grainy, so they could not identify a color. It appeared to be a Ford or another domestic model. They put Lisa in the back seat, and the one who kidnapped her got in the passenger seat. Then, the car pulled away. It was impossible to see the license. It appeared they were headed for the exit. Kellum felt they probably got on the freeway for a quick getaway. He called the station and told Todd what he knew so he could initiate the Amber Alert. It wasn't much, but you never knew. Since the Amber Alert was made into law, hundreds of children have been recovered yearly.

Kellum then called the number he had for his NCSBI contact. "Is this about the abduction?" Keith Victory said when he saw Kellum's number come up.

"You better believe it. Are you on your way?"

"I will contact the FBI, then be on my way. Per protocol, they need to be informed, although I'm sure they know about it by now. Are you at the mall?"

"Yes, and will be here a while. See you soon."

Kellum told the security officer to take him to the lady who was in the bathroom when Lisa was abducted. They walked over to an area roped off with crime scene tape. A woman was sitting there, and she looked shaken. She was dabbing her eyes with a tissue. "Miss, this is Sheriff Taylor, and he would like to ask you a few questions."

Kellum sat next to the woman and quietly introduced himself again. "What is your name, for my records?" he asked her, and he had his pen and notepad ready.

"Kathleen Shaw."

"Thank you. Would you tell me everything you remember seeing or hearing in the bathroom, please," asked Kellum.

"I walked in and went to the stall next to the one at the end. I could see that the one on the other end was occupied. I only noticed that the door appeared closed all the way. Some others had doors partially open, so I thought it was occupied, but I did not hear a thing. I have been wracking my brain trying to think all of this through.

"I put my purse and shopping bags on the back of the door, then unbuttoned my pants. While doing that, my head was down, and that was when they walked out. I don't remember hearing the lavatory used, but I thought nothing of it. Since the pandemic, I have noticed many people use hand sanitizers. I do that sometimes, myself."

"So you didn't hear anyone speak, nor did you see anyone, so you wouldn't be able to say if it was one or two people who left?" Kellum asked.

"That's right. I know now that there were two people, but, like I said, I had my head down about the time they left. I don't remember hearing anything but the shuffling of feet, like someone walking lightly and the door opening and closing."

"Were you still shopping? How did you know about the abduction?"

"Yes, I had several shops to go to. My birthday was last week, and I had some things to return and a few to exchange. My husband doesn't always get my size right, but he tries, at least."

"Thank you, Mrs. Shaw. We will contact you in the future because we will probably need a more formal statement if you can come into the Sheriff's office. If not, we will send an officer to you."

"I'll be happy to come," she said. "I just hope they find this poor girl and there is a happy ending."

After Kellum finished interviewing Mrs. Shaw, he asked the security officer at the video table which girl Lisa gave money to before she went to the bathroom. The officer pointed to a girl sitting at the table in the food court, "The one with dark curly hair and a red top and blue cutoffs."

"Thank you," said Kellum.

He walked over to the table and asked if the girl the security officer pointed out would speak with him. Tiffany stood up, and Kellum offered his hand, introduced himself, and asked her name and age.

"I'm Tiffany Armano, thirteen years old."

"Okay, Tiffany, I would like to ask you some questions. Would that be all right?"

"Sure, I am happy to help," she said nervously.

"Was Lisa going to meet anyone when she gave you money and left the table?"

"No, nothing like that. She only told me to get her a pretzel and a soft drink. She laid a five on the table and walked towards the bathroom."

"Did you see her go into the bathroom?"

"No, I guess I didn't. Is that a problem?"

"No, dear, no problem. I am just asking to clarify. We have video cameras that can verify most of her actions."

"You didn't see her leave the bathroom alone?"

"No, sir. I did not; no one did. It was at least half an hour before we realized she was not back; I was through with my pretzel and noticed hers lying there, which was when it dawned on me. A couple of us ran into the bathroom, but no one was there. We started screaming her name, and a security guard ran up."

"Okay, thank you, Tiffany. I may call on you again later."

"Yes, sir, you're welcome."

chapter 11

Cynthia called her son, Martin, as she left the State House. "Hi, dear. I was wondering if I could stop by on my way home?"

"Sure, Mom, what's the occasion?"

"I got the votes."

Cynthia had persuaded so many Senators about the Bill in committee that her head was spinning. Bar none, she had all the votes she needed to pass the Bill overwhelmingly. She didn't want to brag, but she felt her clout with some of the Senators had something to do with it. Her mother taught her to act like you knew what you were doing, whether you did or not! It was some sage advice, but it often worked.

When she arrived at Martin's office, his assistant told her he was on the phone but wouldn't be long. "Thank you, Mary. I will have a seat here." Cynthia chose a comfortable leather wing chair in the corner. She remembered working with Susan, Martin's wife, to decorate the office.

Martin came to the waiting room a few minutes later and hugged his mother. "Come on in," and they walked into his office.

She plopped down in one of his comfortable chairs, sighed, and said, "It's over and done. The vote has been delayed for two weeks due to a death in the family of one of the Senators, and some of them plan to attend the funeral. These things happen. It's disappointing, but it will be in about two weeks, and there's no doubt the governor will sign."

"We should go and celebrate. Are you free tonight?"

"Could we wait until tomorrow? I am bushed. I still have to run by your house and pick up Missy."

"Sure. Have you heard the news today?"

"No, not really. What's going on?" asked Cynthia.

"Trent Willams' youngest daughter was abducted."

"No," gasped Cynthia. "How? What happened?"

"Apparently, she was taken out of a bathroom from the mall yesterday." The FBI, State police, NCSBI, you name it. They are all on it."

"See, that was why I worked so hard on the bill. I pray she will be found before it's too late. They were sure it was an abduction?"

"They have it all on video, but the problem was that the car plates could not be seen. There wasn't a ransom demand yet, at least none I've heard."

"I don't feel like celebrating now, son. We must support their family and pray for her safe return," said Cynthia.

"I agree, Mother, but we can't let your accomplishment go to waste. We will pray for them, and with your effort, hopefully, it will never happen to another child." Martin stood and walked over to her, and she let him escort her out. He had a lot of work to do to get home at a decent time.

Martin had been an ideal son. He graduated valedictorian from high school and attended the University of North Carolina, Chapel Hill. He majored in history and minored in political science. He enjoyed his law practice and never had any call to seek political office. He had enough business and repeat business to keep him busy for many years. Lately, however, he was considering at least a school board run with the political climate being what it was. A group from his daughter's school approached him to do so. Their girls were being home-schooled at the present, but only because of COVID-19.

They were devastated when he and his wife realized what was happening in their public school. The graphic library books showed genitalia and cartoon characters that portrayed that they could be any sex they wanted to be. The teachers were mandated to use the pronouns the school deemed appropriate according to the child. It was too much. His wife, Susan, graduated with a teaching degree from Appalachian State. She was qualified to teach preschool through fifth grade. So they pulled them out of school, and she started homeschooling. It had made all the difference.

Their girls were beautifully behaved and good students. His wife made sure they were good with their studies and also extra curricular activities. He was a lucky man and he knew it. The thought of one of them ever being abducted made him physically ill.

Cynthia drove to her son's house and was greeted by Missy when she walked in the back door. She jumped up and down like she had not seen her for days. Missy was a loving dog, and she wanted to be with her as much as possible, preferably in her lap. All of her granddaughters came running to see her. She hugged them, sat down, and asked them to tell her what they were doing this summer.

Susan, their mom, walked into the room and said, "Tell Grandmama what you all are doing."

Elizabeth started. "I am going to a sewing class. A lady in our neighborhood is teaching it. I am learning how to sew on buttons, and next, she will teach me how to hem a skirt. We won't be using the machine for a while."

Nicole was next. "I am taking swimming lessons and a first aid course. I'll be able to help someone if they are drowned."

Susan corrected her grammar, "You mean if they are drowning, but let's hope that doesn't happen."

Nicole said, "That's right. I don't want anyone to die."

Her grandmother laughed at that, which Nicole thought was cruel. "You don't want anyone to die, do you?" she asked.

"No, of course not, Nicole. I'm sorry if it sounded like that."

Courtney, the youngest, piped up and said, "I am learning how to play the piano."

Even though she already knew what they were all doing, Cynthia feigned her satisfaction. Martin had told her all of their planned activities before. "Well, I am so glad my girls are learning something besides old reading, writing, and arithmetic this summer," said Cynthia.

Susan said, "It keeps them busy, and I have to keep a schedule taped to the fridge to keep up with it all."

"I better get going." As they walked to the door, Cynthia said, "Martin told me he wanted to celebrate my accomplishment tomorrow night. Will that be okay with you, Susan? Of course, I feel bad about celebrating anything now."

"Do you mean what I think you mean, the Williams girl?"

"Yes, so sad for that family."

"I do feel bad for them, but you have quite an accomplishment to celebrate, and I think we should honor you for it. I will call my usual sitter and make sure she is available. If not, do you mind if the girls come?"

"You know I would love for my grands to be there. Why don't we make it a family affair and do something they would like?"

"Do you mean McDonald's?" said Susan, laughing.

"I'm not sure we should go that far; see if they would agree to Sergio's? They have a kid's menu."

"Sure, they will be fine. It's a good place with a lot of ambiance," agreed Susan.

"Come, come, Missy girl. Let's go home so I can get a relaxing bath," called Cynthia while her Maltese ran with the girls following behind her.

chapter

12

Angela helped get Andy ready for bed. She was supposed to go out with Brent tonight, but her mother had to work an extra shift, so she canceled. She didn't mind, though. *Dateline* was on tonight, and she always enjoyed watching it.

Dateline had already started by the time she got settled in. She watched it as long as she could but finally succumbed to sleep. It was about a husband suspected of killing his wife, what a lot of them were about, sadly. Her mom arrived home at eleven and woke her up. When she got her bearings, she saw that her mom must have turned off the TV. Now, she was wondering what happened. *Did he do it?* She knew she could look it up tomorrow to find out.

"Let's get you to bed," her mom said, holding her arm and returning to her bedroom. Andy's door was open, so she knew her mom had already checked on him because she had closed it so the TV wouldn't wake him. She already had her nightshirt on, so she crawled into her bed and fell fast asleep.

Brenda went to the bathroom, removed her waitress uniform, and showered. Afterward, she went to the kitchen, poured herself a bowl of Raisin Bran, and used the rest of the milk. She realized she would need to run to the closest market in the morning and get milk for Andy. She was dead tired after her double shift but needed the money, and the tips were better at night. A handsome man came in tonight and flirted with her.

She had never seen him before and wondered if he moved here recently. When he left, she saw him get into a black F150; it looked like a newer model. She wondered if he was a builder scouting the area to buy land. There was so much building around this area that it was hard to keep up.

She finished her cereal while watching *Jimmy Kimmell* but was getting so sleepy she could hardly keep her eyes open. She returned to the kitchen, rinsed the cereal bowl, and put it in the dishwasher. She got in bed and hoped to dream of the handsome man she had waited on, and just as she was dozing off, she wondered what it would be like to be married to someone like that so she could stop working.

The following day, Angela got up early. She decided to let her mom sleep in, so she tip-toed by her door to the kitchen. She looked in the fridge and realized they were out of milk. Even though she didn't have her license yet, she was tempted to drive to the nearest market and pick some up for Andy's cereal, but she thought better of it because if something were to happen, it would be such a hardship on her mother that she may never recover. She knew how to drive but had to take driver's education when school started back to get a discount on the insurance she knew her mom would have to pay.

She knew how to scramble eggs, so if Andy got up before her mom, she would make him some. She wished her mom would start buying Pop-Tarts again for Andy, but she refused, saying they are bad for you, and she wanted her children to begin eating healthier foods. Angela wondered how long it would last, but her mom surprised her and had stuck with the plan for almost a year. She made a piece of toast and put some peanut butter on it. That usually held her for several hours.

She checked her phone and found several texts from Brent, asking her to contact him immediately. He mentioned that it was about his sister, Lisa. She knew Lisa was always getting into trouble, so she didn't think that much of it, but since he had sent her three texts, she decided it might be important. She called his number even though it was still early.

"You are not going to believe this: Lisa is missing," he said when he answered.

"Missing, what? Oh, come on." She thought he was pulling her leg.

"She was kidnapped from the shopping mall. I'm surprised you didn't see it on the news," Brent said.

"I fell asleep during *Dateline* and just got up. My mom must not have seen it yet because she would have awakened me. What can I do?"

"I don't know. The police are all over our house. The mall was closed. They have the kidnapping on videotape and even the car they put her in. However, the tape was black and white and grainy, so they couldn't make out the color and didn't have the plates. I'm really worried about my parents. Linda was notified last night and was on her way home from school."

"I will tell my mom. Maybe you could pick me up for some company and support?"

"Yeah, sounds good. Call me."

"Okay," said Angela, adding, "I'm so sorry."

Andy came dragging himself into the kitchen. "Hey, little brother." Angela got up and hugged him. "Can I make you some eggs? We don't have any milk, sorry."

"Sure, please make me two eggs, and can I have some toast and jelly?" asked Andy.

"You've got it, little guy," said Angela.

Angela cleaned the kitchen and emptied the trash after sweeping the floor. She knew her mom would be tired and thought she should help her today. She planned to clean her room and do some laundry.

Dating Brent caused her to get behind in her responsibilities around the house. She appreciated that her mother didn't fuss at her too much.

Her girlfriend, Monique, started dating way too early. Her mother did her best to keep her on the straight and narrow, but Monique thought she knew best. Now, she had a two-year-old and had dropped out of school. Her boyfriend, whom she believed loved her, ditched her as soon as she told him she was pregnant, and she hadn't seen him since.

Her mother and stepfather were helping to raise little Davey; Monique named him after her birth father, who left her mother after she was born. It was kind of a slap in the face to her stepfather, but he accepted it and raised Davey like he was his grandson. She believed Monique had second thoughts about his name, but she probably had second thoughts about many things.

When Angela's mom got up, she told her about Lisa. "That's awful, I'm so sorry. Please be careful, Angela. There are creeps out there."

"I know, mom. Would it be okay for me to spend some time with Brent? He's so upset and could use my support."

"Of course, baby."

chapter

13

Angela knew Lisa had a wild side to her. Brent had expressed his concern for her before. But she knew he didn't see this coming, abducted; who would have thought that would happen in their little town? She wondered if whoever did it knew how promiscuous she was and perhaps just wanted to have their way with her. She shook her head to get that thought out of her head. She couldn't help but believe they abducted her because they knew her family. Perhaps a ransom?

She knew the Williams family had a lot of money, but they were working folks; it wasn't like they were super wealthy. She prayed the police were on top of it by now and that she would be found soon.

"Angela, Brent is pulling up outside," her mother called out to her. She grabbed her purse and went out to the living room area. Andy was watching cartoons on television. She gave him a kiss on his cheek. He lifted his head and gave her a kiss on her chin. It tickled her, and she rubbed where he had planted the kiss and smiled at him. "I love you," she told him.

"Mom, I'm sorry. I haven't gotten my room cleaned yet. I cleaned and swept the kitchen, and I'll do my room later."

"Don't worry about it." Brenda came over, kissed her daughter on the cheek, and hugged her.

Brent came to the front door, and Angela was there right away to let him in. Then she hugged him. He said hello to Angela's mother and brother before they left to drive to his house. He filled her in on what they knew so far.

"Sheriff Taylor called in the FBI, the NCSBI, the county deputies, and all the surrounding counties are working around the clock. They set up phone equipment at our house in case of a ransom. So far, no calls."

"How are your parents?" Angela asked, concerned.

"My mom is a wreck. Linda got here a little while ago, so that will help. Everyone is still in shock. Something I haven't told you yet: they have a video of when she was removed from the mall."

"Oh, wow. How did they do it?"

"One of them dressed her in a bathroom near the food court close to an exit door. They put a large shawl around her and a wig and hat. Apparently, she was drugged because you could see she wasn't walking well. The person who was in disguise was dragging her across the floor. The outside cameras show her being put in the backseat of an older model car. I think it's a Ford Taurus. The footage was grainy, so the video wasn't beneficial. The driver took off as soon as his buddy hopped in the front seat. The cameras show them exiting toward the freeway. They tried to get the plate but could not see it. They feel like it was a stolen car, anyway. So, they probably got on the highway, and who knows where they went from there."

"I hate to say it, but this sounds like something you would see on a *Dateline* episode. I'm not trying to minimize it; I apologize if it sounded that way." She reached over and squeezed his hand.

"No need to apologize. We are living one of those episodes."

"How would they know which one of those girls to kidnap and that they would be going into a bathroom?" asked Angela.

"That's an excellent question. I hadn't thought of that. It was probably just random, I think. If two of them came in the bathroom, that probably would have stopped them, but we may never know."

"There is safety in numbers," said Angela, and Brent nodded.

When they arrived, Angela entered the house and went straight to Mrs. Williams. "I'm so sorry you all are going through this. What can I do to help you?"

"Please just help Brent get through this," replied Brent's mother with tears in her eyes.

"Yes, ma'am. I plan to help him, but I can also help you. My mom was also distraught and would like to do something."

Angela saw several casserole dishes on the large island that had not been put away. She assumed they had been dropped off just this morning. She told Mrs. Williams she would be glad to make a list of the food items and what type of container they are in so she can get the containers back to the right people. "Would that help you now?"

"Yes, it would. I didn't even think about that. Thank you, Angela."

Angela started methodically making a list of each dish, who brought it, and what kind of container it was in. After she got everything caught up, she accepted the food as it came in and kept the list going. Linda, Brent's sister, came into the kitchen, and she showed her what she had done so she could take over after she left.

Sheriff Taylor came into the kitchen and introduced himself to Angela. "Did you know Lisa?"

"Not well, but yes, from school. I'm so sorry this is happening. I'll be glad to help in any way I can. Brent is my boyfriend, and I care for him and his family," said Angela.

"I'm sure that is comforting," Kellum told her. Then he left to return to the front of the house.

Angela suddenly heard a lot of activity and saw people with FBI jackets taking computers out of the house. She presumed they had to look at everything. It was like a CSI episode. She told herself to snap out of it; *this was real life.*

Brent returned to the kitchen and told her he was going with his dad to see the scene at the mall. He asked if she wanted to come. "Sure, I'll call my mom and let her know."

Angela texted her mother instead, letting her know she would be home later and where she was going. Her mom acknowledged the message and texted that she had made a lasagna so Brent could take it back when he brought her home. Angela texted her back and told her that was nice and that they would enjoy it.

Mr. Willams was solemn on the ride to the mall. Angela sat in the backseat. She told him how sorry she and her family were, and she was praying for Lisa. He acknowledged her sentiments and thanked her for the prayers.

Trent told his son, "I got a call this morning from the new cousin I met a couple of weeks ago, Brent. You remember the one with the catering business, Gene Talbot?"

"Yes, I remember him. He was nice and very interesting. What did he say?"

"Of course, he said he was concerned, that he was praying for Lisa and us and that we should let him know if we needed anything. There is nothing anyone can do except pray," said Trent.

"Dad, Angela asked a great question this morning. Did the abductors know who they were kidnapping, or would they have taken any of those girls? Was it a random thing; if not, how could they be sure Lisa would go to the bathroom?"

"Those are great questions and ones we need to ask Sheriff Taylor," said Trent.

chapter

14

Gene had gotten home around ten o'clock in the evening. Tonight's event was a going away party in Leland for Judy Morrow, a woman he had known since starting his business. She helped him when he first got started. He met her at the local college while taking culinary classes. She was newly retired and bored because her husband played golf almost daily, and she was tired of playing cards and Mah Jong. He had to ask her what Mah Jong was, and she filled him in. "I'll teach you how to play if you want."

That was when he told her he was starting a business and didn't have time. He wanted to add "for frivolous things," but he thought better and asked if she would like to help him with the catering. "I could use a woman's touch, especially with food selections." It was a lucky ask because Judy was dying to do something creative. She had worked as a paralegal in Wilmington for over twenty years and was tired of being holed up in an office and courtroom daily. "I'll work for free; just give me an opportunity."

Gene told her he couldn't let her do that, but they worked out a schedule and a small salary that satisfied them. She was so detail-oriented that she quickly got his business up and running. She even spoke to the attorney with whom she had primarily worked and talked him into doing pro-bono work for Gene. So, he got his contracts for the business written by an attorney at no cost to him.

She worked for him for three years, then decided to spend more time traveling with her husband. Last year, he passed away from a sudden heart attack. She recently decided to sell her house and move back to New Jersey, where she was from. She wanted to be close to her children and grandchildren. Her friends and neighbors threw her a big going away party, and of course, they had Gene cater it since she had been instrumental in getting his business started. He thanked her again for all she had done for him and promised to stay in touch. She was wonderful, and he would never forget what she had done for him. She even helped him find Sara, which had worked out very well.

Gene turned on the eleven o'clock news station out of Raleigh and caught the story of the abduction of a thirteen-year-old girl named Lisa Williams. He wondered if she could be the daughter of his cousin he just met recently. He remembered when he showed him pictures of his daughters. His son, Brent, was there with him, and he seemed like a good kid. His wife, Michelle, couldn't join them because she promised to do something with their oldest daughter, who was in college. The broadcast showed the distraught parents pleading for her safe return; he saw Trent and knew.

Later that day, before he went to the evening catering job, he called his cousin as a courtesy. He spoke with Trent for about ten minutes, offering any assistance, even money for a reward, but Trent told him they had all that covered. The police were on it and had called in the NCSBI and the FBI. He told him he appreciated the call and asked for prayers. Gene told him he would pray for him and his family. After the call, he still felt terrible. He never had children but couldn't imagine the suffering that you would go through if you had a child disappear, especially under these circumstances. He remembered how Ally helped the Morgans when their daughter's skeletal remains were found on the beach nearby. Her disappearance was thirty years before that, but the pain was the same as if she had just gone missing that same day. Ally remained close to them. He had catered Mr. Morgan's birthday party about a week ago. Ally told him everyone enjoyed the food and let Marie know. She boasted about knowing Ally, which was how she knew about Gene. He thought he would get some catering jobs out of that connection.

When he arrived at the wedding reception that evening, he was tired. They had worked nonstop for the last eight days except Sunday, and he felt he needed a break. He tries not to work Sundays, but in the busy season, it is sometimes unavoidable. He planned to ask Sara to carve out some time in the next few weeks, even if she had to turn away business. He thinks it would be an excellent time to visit his new cousin and help with the search.

Eliza arrived early and was helping set up inside. She approached Gene and asked if she could have some time off due to a trip, she wanted to take with her daughter to look at colleges in the fall. "I hate to do that to you since you are a little short-handed, but it was important to her, and Jack can't leave his business right now."

Gene knew Jack was her husband, and he had an auto shop business in Wilmington. Eliza had shared with Gene a while back that they had some marital issues to work out. Apparently, they had worked them out because they planned a cruise in January. He thought it might be a big anniversary they were celebrating.

"No worries," Gene told her. I am thinking about taking some time off, too. Then he told her about the abduction of his second cousin, a thirteen-year-old girl.

"Really?" asked Eliza. "I have something I need to tell you, Gene."

"What is it? Did it happen in your family?"

Eliza looked serious and said, "Gene, I work for you part-time for a reason. I'm an undercover FBI agent, primarily in the human trafficking division."

Gene's jaw dropped. He couldn't get the words out but finally said, "Are you telling me you suspect that I'm a human trafficker?"

Eliza looked shocked and quickly explained. "Oh, heavens no. I'm sorry you took it that way. I don't always work for you. I have a couple of other part-time jobs as an undercover operator. The FBI has been infiltrating agents into jobs in the field to seek out child predators, offenders, and groomers. It's a huge business, Gene. I know people want to think the best of their fellow man, but I'm here to tell you that many bad actors are out there just waiting to jump on the opportunity to traffic a child."

"Are you going to be brought into this case? I would like it if you were."

"I don't know since it's not my territory, but it could fall in my area of expertise; if it is a sex traffic case, I would probably be asked to help. In that case, my daughter will have to wait for the trip to see colleges. I will call my supervisor and see what I can find out. Let's get through this job, then we'll talk. Oh, one more thing, I have told you this in confidence, so I hope you understand that my cover must not be blown."

"So, technically, you are working as an agent now?" asked Gene.

"So, technically, the answer is yes," she winked at him.

Once the wedding reception was done and they were packed up, Eliza approached Gene. She told him confidentially, "I just got a message that I am scheduled for a meeting at the Sheriff's office in Blaylock County tomorrow morning at nine. Please remove me from the schedule for a while. I guess my daughter's college trip will have to wait."

chapter

15

"Leave me alone, damn you to hell," Lisa screamed at Walter. "I told you I don't want any food. I want to go home, and I mean now."

"Screaming is not going to do you any good. No one can hear you. You might as well eat."

It had been twenty-four hours, and Lisa hadn't eaten anything since they brought her here. She had refused to drink, and to his knowledge, she had not urinated.

"You will be sick and dehydrated if you don't eat and drink."

She kicked the plate with her bound feet across the room, with food flying everywhere. Walter got so mad with her that he almost slapped her, but he didn't want to be seen on tape doing that. He knew the video feed was going to their boss's laptop.

He left the plate and the food so she could see what she had done and returned upstairs. He said to Vinnie, "You can try next time. I've had it with her."

"With any luck, the boss man will be coming tonight to pick her up. He told me to prepare her for transport in the next four hours a little while ago. So I am thinking between ten and eleven tonight," said Vinnie.

They had been watching the news, and the coverage had been extensive. The national media had picked it up. There was a CNN set up at the mall as well as NBC. The press had found out who she was, and now they wondered if this had been the one pitfall in their plan. Why couldn't they have found someone from a broken home with a mother who was a drug addict? Life would be so much easier right now. They were having a hard time getting close enough to her to give her another shot. She was so strong and had such long legs; she kicked anytime they got within a few feet of her. Vinnie knew they would have to go down and give her a shot when he got the call about the transport arriving. It was just a matter of time. *Good luck to the bloke that had to take her from here,* Vinnie thought.

They heard the name Lisa Williams on the small TV, another news story about the abduction. They were now showing the video of the kidnapping, and Walter got close to the screen to make sure they could not see his face. He was pleasantly surprised when he could not even recognize himself. The next scene was her parents and her brother and sister in front of their house, begging for the safe return of their daughter. The mother looked as white as a ghost and as if she could collapse any minute. Walter actually felt terrible for her. But then he snapped out of it when he heard Vinnie's cell phone receive a notification.

Vinnie looked at him and said, "They'll be here in an hour."

Walter got the syringe ready. They wanted to time it just right. Vinnie suggested they attack her at the same time, and since Walter was larger, he was going to sit on her legs. He can inject the medication if Vinnie can get her flipped on her side. They know it will keep her out for at least an hour. The boss's man will text them within fifteen minutes of arriving.

In the meantime, Walter went downstairs, taking a mop and bucket along. He knew he would have to be the one to clean up the mess their kidnap victim had made. He unlocked the door, and Lisa was ready for him. She reached for the fork that had fallen off the plate with her toes when she kicked it. Walter had not seen it. She used it to cut the flex cuff enough to get it off her feet, and then she got out of the wrist cuff. When Walter walked into the room, she hit him in the head and used the fork to manage to punch his left eye. He screamed while raising both hands to his eye. She exited the room, trying to find the way out, and once she did, she ran toward it.

Vinnie heard Walter scream, and he came running downstairs with a syringe in hand, caught her at the door, and jabbed her right buttock before she turned around. She immediately went limp in his arms, and he let her down to the floor. He ran into the basement room where they held her to find Walter dazed and bleeding profusely from his left eye. He was sitting on the bed and rocking back and forth. Vinnie knew he had left his phone upstairs and wanted to get Walter medical help, so he ran back upstairs, grabbed a dish towel, and loaded it with several ice cubes. He picked up his phone and ran back downstairs. He saw Lisa lying on the floor, still unconscious, so he ran into the room and put ice on Walter's eye. His cell phone vibrated, and it had a message reading: 5 min away. *Thank goodness*, he thought.

He told Walter to stay as still as possible and had him lower the ice pack so he could visualize the eye. It appeared she grazed the outside but did not damage the eye. *Lucky break*, he thought. "They are going to be here any minute to get the wildcat. Just stay still, and I will come back to you. She's knocked out, so our work is almost done."

"Okay," said Walter.

Vinnie heard the van coming into the driveway. He ran back upstairs and saw from the front window that it was backing up, which was good. That way, no one could see from the street that the girl was being loaded in the bay. He went outside once the van stopped and the driver's door opened. "Hi, I'm Vinnie."

"George, and this is my brother Rob." Rob went to the back and opened the van's doors. Vinnie could see there was a makeshift cot with some handcuffs attached.

"My partner and I just had a nasty run-in with her. Somehow, she detached from the flex cuffs; we don't know how, probably an eating utensil from when she kicked her plate across the room. She jabbed my partner in the eye with something, maybe a fork, but luckily, it didn't appear that the eye was damaged. She tried to get out the back door, but I made it to her in time to give her a shot, so she was knocked out. Just make sure she is well secured. She's a wild one and very strong."

"Thanks for the warning. Can you help us get her loaded?"

"Sure thing, right this way." Vinnie led them down the basement stairs. They picked her up, carried her up the stairs, and got her in the van bay without incident.

"She is easy when she isn't a bucking broncho," Vinnie told them.

The van left, and Vinnie went back downstairs to take care of Walter and finish cleaning up. Once they were out of there, they would hole up at a Ramada Inn near the airport. Their boss wanted them to lay low for a week. The room was already reserved and paid for, according to the boss.

chapter 16

Angela was glad to be home. It had been a long couple of days. She returned to Brent's, helped answer calls, and assisted Linda and her aunt in any way she could. Brent and his dad spent the day talking on the front porch. There had been no news from the Amber Alert, and the videos didn't pan out either, although the police were still looking and following up on tips.

He told her, "If only I had paid more attention, perhaps I could have prevented it."

She told him, "It's not your fault, Brent. Lisa was headstrong. She's always been that way. What would you have been able to do to prevent this from happening? I'm sure it was random; she was just an easy target at the wrong place and time."

"I know, but my parents are brokenhearted and won't ever get over this."

"There's still a chance she will be found. They have more help coming. I overheard the sheriff talking with your father. Something about an FBI agent who specializes in sex trafficking, and she was in NC and will be here in the morning."

Before Brent left, he told Brenda how much they appreciated the lasagna she had made for them. He kissed Angela on the cheek. "I'll call you tomorrow."

"Drive carefully, please," said Angela.

Angela was restless the rest of the evening and had trouble sleeping. Once she did, she dreamed that two men were talking about a young girl. She heard 'she was perfect' in her sleep, but 'they needed to do it soon.' She dreamed she heard two car doors and the cars cranking, then passed out. She was in such a deep sleep when she awoke the next morning, still in a fog.

"Are you okay?" asked her mom. "What do you mean?"

"You just look like you're still half asleep. You're usually so chipper in the morning. Are you sick?" Brenda asked.

"No, I don't think so, but I feel odd. Can I go lie down for a while more?"

"Of course, let me know if you need anything. I am not going in to work until noon."

Angela went back to her room. She looked in on Andy, who was sound asleep. She lay down and tried to remember what she had dreamed of last night because she thought that was what was bugging her.

"Oh my God," she screamed out.

Her mother came running in, and so did Andy. Her scream awakened him and scared him so badly.

"I just remembered something I overheard. Do you remember the night I came home and I had slipped and hit my head, and Brent thought I had a concussion?"

"Yes."

"Well, I am sure now that I overheard two men talking. I think I heard them planning to abduct someone, but I didn't know quite what they were talking about. Since Lisa was missing, I'm sure that was what I heard. I dreamt it last night, which was why I felt so odd. I remember something. I have to tell someone right away. Please call Brent for me."

"Okay, where is your phone?"

"Over by the window being charged."

Brenda got the phone and gave it to Angela. Angela called Brent and screamed, "Please get over here now. I have something to tell you. Bring the police."

"What is it?" asked Brent.

Angela handed the phone to her mother.

"Brent, this is Brenda. Angela had a terrible dream last night, and I think she is having some dream or remembrance from the night she hit her head. I think y'all need to get here as soon as possible. I don't want her to suppress whatever it is."

Brent ran to his father's study and told him they needed to get to Angela's house and take a detective or policeman.

"Why, what is going on? Are they hurt, or is she missing now?" asked Trent. He could see the panic in his son's eyes.

"No, nothing like that. It's a long story, but remember the night I came home and told you Angela had had an accidental fall, and I had trouble finding her. Then I was worried she had a concussion?"

"Yes, I remember."

"Well, her mother just called and said Angela woke up screaming that she remembered something about that night. She's insistent that it has something to do with Lisa."

Trent called Sheriff Taylor, who told him he would meet him there. He said he would bring the new FBI agent who arrived that morning: Eliza Mancini. He planned to brief her on the way.

Brent and his father arrived first. Brenda had coffee ready for them. Angela was on the sofa curled up, her knees tight to her chest. She was in a trance. Brent walked over to her and asked if she was okay. She just stared at him and nodded her head.

"Son, let's wait until Sheriff Taylor gets here so he can question her. He will know how to handle this."

"Yes, sir," said Brent.

It wasn't long before the Sheriff knocked on the door. Trent opened the door and let him in, along with the FBI agent. She was introduced to everyone and sat on the sofa beside Angela. Sheriff Taylor pulled up a kitchen chair that Brenda had brought over for him. Brent and his dad stood to the side and tried to stay out of sight.

"Angela, would you please tell me and Sheriff Taylor what was troubling you this morning? Was it a dream or something you recalled?"

Angela looked at Eliza and said, "I heard two men talking, and they were discussing taking a girl. They said the selection was right but needed to be done soon because time was running out. They said something about talking to the boss. Then I heard two doors shut and two cars turned on. One sounded like a truck. My boyfriend owns one," she said.

She looked up at Brent and said, "I thought it sounded like his truck."

"Okay, that's great information. Would you tell me precisely when this was, and was this the first time you recall hearing it?"

Brent said, "It was a week ago, last Tuesday night. I remember because there was a Braves game that night, and I finished watching it when I got home. I was worried about Angela, though, after her fall."

Brenda then spoke up and said, "That is right, I didn't work that night, and when she got home, she had a slight bump on the back of her head. I sat up with her for as long as possible, and then we both slept in her bed. As far as I know, she hadn't had any problems since then, at least until this morning."

Eliza looked at Angela, and she nodded in unison. "Okay, that information helps us a lot. Sheriff, we should return to the station and devise some plans. One last thing, did you see the color of the vehicles?"

Angela shook her head and said, "I think black, but they could have just been dark colors. There was no moon to speak of, and except for the bright stars, it was dark with all of the trees. I had walked down the path from where we were to use the bathroom, and that was when I overheard everything. I don't believe they saw me, and I couldn't see them because the trees and all were so thick with leaves."

"Thank you, Angela. You were very brave in coming forth with this information. You rest now. I'm sure the dream wasn't pleasant, but please call if you remember anything else, okay?" she looked up at Brenda when she said this, and Brenda nodded.

chapter

17

After Kellum and Eliza left the house, Eliza asked him, "Do you know this girl well?"

"Not well, no, but I know Brent, and he's a great guy, just like his dad. Do you have any doubts about what she said?"

"No, not really. I wanted to make sure that you didn't. The first thing we need to do is go out to where they were that night, but in the meantime, we need to get a couple of people looking up all the trucks in the county. I think that would be easier than looking for a dark car. Anyway, it's a start."

When they got back to the station, the FBI agent in charge was there, and they filled him in. "I agree with you, Eliza. I will get some reinforcements involved in going through motor vehicle records. Let's pinpoint the area and see where we can locate cameras. By the way, Keith left since I arrived, and we have Eliza, but he will assist in any way he can."

Kellum called Trent on his cell phone. "Can you talk?"

"Yes, I am walking out on the deck," said Trent.

"Good, find out from Brent exactly where they were last Tuesday night. He will probably have to drive there with us. We are going to hunt for cameras today."

"I'll call you right back." Trent walked into the house and told Brent he needed to speak with him. When Brent got up, he told Angela, "I'll be right back, don't worry."

"Yes, Dad, what is it?"

"We need to take the Sheriff and probably a couple of deputies out to the site where you and Angela were the night she fell. You are going to have to show them where you found her. Do you think you can do that?"

"Absolutely; let me tell her where I am going."

After telling Brenda and Angela that he needed to leave to take the officers to the site where they were that night, he rubbed Andy's thick head of hair and said, "Take care of your big sis, okay?"

Andy looked up admiringly at Brent and nodded his head. Angela saw Andy's reaction and thought that it was so sweet.

Brent drove, and his dad rode with him. They met up with the sheriff and three of his officers on the way. They were in two cars. They arrived at the clearing, and he led them down a small hill, where he found Angela. "She could have heard voices anywhere around here, and you know how they carry. She said she could tell they were close to their cars since she heard the doors open and close and then heard two engines being turned on shortly after hearing the conversation. Perhaps they were on a road down the hill. It probably was the road just beyond here."

Kellum told Turner, "How about driving farther up the road we turned off and see if there is another road to go down? We will wait here and see if we hear you come up."

Turner was headed to the cruiser as the sheriff was still giving instructions. He held a thumb up before he took off. They could hear the car coming down the road a few minutes later. It wasn't that far away, but many trees and underbrush were camouflaging the road. Turner called Kellum's cell and asked if he could see him. "Yes, you found it. Keep going down to see if there are any houses. I kind of doubt it. I believe I know where the road goes."

It wasn't long before Turner came back. He told the sheriff that he didn't see any houses or dwellings. He said he had to go quite a long way to find a dirt road to turn around. There was a gate that was locked, and it had a no-trespassing sign.

"Well, we will be checking that out. I need to get back to look at the county and property maps," said Kellum.

Kellum approached Trent and asked, "You know that question you asked me yesterday about how they knew to take Lisa?"

"Yes."

"I think they were tracking her and may have been for a while."

"Why do you think that?"

"It's the only thing that makes sense since Angela told us what she overheard."

On the ride back home, Trent broke down in the truck. "I'm sorry, son, I just hate this. Your mother is about to have a breakdown, and Linda is always crying. I feel helpless. I have to be doing something to help."

"It's okay, Dad. Let's help with the cameras. That can't be that hard. We can offer to go out with another officer. Maybe get deputized? I'm sure they could use extra eyes. Linda's helping Tiffany put up posters, and they have been posting information on social media. That's something, too."

"It sure is," agreed Trent.

Kellum drove to the mall and spoke with the manager. CSI had done its part during the last two days, and the FBI had given him the green light to reopen the mall.

There was a press conference scheduled for noon today. He hadn't had to do many of them in his career, especially since he moved here. The entire complement of law enforcement was going to be there. There would be a lot of media, and he knew many questions would be asked. The public had a right to learn what was happening, so he didn't mind doing it.

He arrived back at the station where Eliza and Agent Camp were strategizing. His assistant told him the mom-and-pop motel down the road was opening its small conference room to use as a staging area for searchers and for out-of-towners to stay. They offered them a cut rate on the room bill.

"Any luck on finding trucks?" he chuckled but in a serious way. Eliza looked up at him like he was crazy. "I was kidding, you know that?"

"Yeah, I know," said Eliza. "The staff is reviewing the records and ruling out all they can, but it is still a massive list. If they were planning on moving her, I am sure it's in the works. Were they putting her on a vessel or taking her by car? This area is a thoroughfare for human traffickers, primarily sex trafficking. Myrtle Beach is a hot spot down in Horry County. There are multiple ways for these scumbags to get these poor victims out of here. Our best bet is to find these guys that kidnapped her and get them talking. We know they are not the actual moneymen. From what Angela said, they had a boss man to answer to. Have you had a chance to check out that property that had the No Trespassing sign on it?"

Kellum said, "No, but it is no problem; I have the maps and records here." He walked over to a shelf in his office and pulled out some maps and county records of property ownership. Finding the property he was looking for took him a few minutes.

"Let's see. We turned off Hwy 408 on a county road. Down from that was a road called Supe's Creek, where Turner turned." He traced his finger and saw several turn-offs, but it looked like the entire property belonged to Jeffrey Edwards.

Agent Camp said, "I'll look him up on my laptop, give me a second."

Kellum told them, "I don't recognize that name, but we have a lot of people that invest in the land around here for hunting and just investment and speculation."

"I've got him. He's a hedge fund manager with a firm out of New York. Global Track Securities. It appears he lives in Raleigh, like you said, Sheriff Taylor. I don't show a truck, but he owns a black Mercedes

550SL. His wife is Stella Bernstock Edwards. His net worth is $35 million. The guy must make some serious dough. But it gets better; his wife is an heiress to the cosmetic company, Bernstock, with an estimated net worth of $100 million, so he married money."

"I think we need to make a house call on Mr. Edwards. The news conference is at noon, which gives us two hours."

He said to his assistant, "Sheila, would you please contact the press and postpone until two? Call all the parties involved. I may be tied up a little longer."

chapter

18

Ally and Neal were disembarking at the Myrtle Beach Airport. They had flown to Bartow to see her parents, and it was a great trip. They flew into Orlando and rented a car to drive to Bartow. Her mother showed them around the small, quaint town. Even though Ally had been there before, she enjoyed seeing it again with Neal. Her mother showed them the house used in the movie *My Girl*.

Her dad was doing great. He had some signs of dementia but generally was functional. Her mother didn't seem over-taxed, so she was glad to see that.

Neal and her dad grilled steaks and talked politics. Ally's mom was unusually cheerful. Ally thinks her mom was happy that perhaps she had found someone to be with, and then she would have all her little ducklings taken care of. She saw her brother and his girlfriend, Greta, one evening. They met them at a restaurant in Tampa. Her parents chose to stay home. They enjoyed their visit, and since Craig was a Physician's Assistant in Sports Medicine, he and Neal had much to discuss. Greta was a teacher at a private school.

Ally asked Greta if the pandemic had hurt them, but Greta said no. "Our enrollment is up. If you know what I mean, people are sick of the public school system and want their children in a more normal environment, one they grew up in."

"I do indeed. I heard about it on the news. I don't think it's as bad in my area yet, but it probably will be soon. With the open border, there is no telling what we will see."

A tropical storm was brewing and threatening the Gulf area, so they cut their trip short by a day. She was sad to have to do that, but they all understood. Her parents were inland far enough that they were not worried about it. Craig and Greta were brave enough to ride it out. The problem was if they didn't leave when they did, they could have been delayed several days, and Neal could not afford to do that. So, when they returned to Myrtle, they decided to check into a hotel there for a night. Ally's friend, Mary, was taking care of Lucky. She called and told her they were okay but would wait another day.

After they landed, Ally called Three Island Catering, and Gene answered and told her they were busy and that it would be appreciated if she could plan to work the following night. He told her he 'lost' Eliza for a few weeks but didn't elaborate. "Sure, just text me the details, and I will help, no worries."

They checked into a high-rise hotel, The Pelican's Nest. While with her parents, they slept in the same room because they only had one guest room. Their third room was an office. But they were polite, and there was no wild sex. Ally felt funny even though she was a grown woman. "It's just not right," she told Neal, laughing.

They made up for it as soon as they checked in and then dressed to go to dinner. He took her to the same restaurant they visited when Deidra and Edward were here almost two years ago. It was as good as it had been then.

They both had the grouper and shared a bottle of Josh Cellars chardonnay.

"I wonder why Eliza had to take so much time off suddenly?" she asked rhetorically. "I always felt she needed the job; I thought her husband was self-employed, and she had a daughter about to graduate high school. But what do I know?"

"Maybe it was a family emergency; you never know," Neal commented.

"That's true. I should mind my business. I have enough of it." She decided to shut up about work then.

They drove back to the hotel and took a walk on the beach. There were many people since it was summer, but they managed around all of the skimpily-clad people to find a walking area. "I wonder if these young people have any idea what they are doing to their skin?" asked Ally.

Neal laughed, "Did you when you were their age?"

"Yes, actually, but the tan was more important," she admitted.

When they got back in the room, Ally turned on the news, and she saw a story about a teenage girl being abducted in North Carolina.

They were showing a press conference that was held earlier that day. The sheriff gave an update, but it was not good news. He stated they had a few trackable clues and encouraged any tips to be called in, no matter how minor. He emphasized there were FBI agents on the case, and every officer in the county was helping. "We are dedicated to finding this young lady." A phone number at the bottom of the screen was the tip line. The area was unfamiliar to her, but when they said the name of the missing girl, Lisa Williams, Ally remembered Gene mentioning the name of one of the cousins with whom he had recently connected. She was sure the last name was Williams. *Could this be the same family?* She wondered.

Neal was in a frisky mood. Their pre-dinner sex had not been enough, so he immediately spooned with her when they crawled into bed. Ally had worn a skimpy gown, left over from her New York single years. It didn't take him long to get it over her head, and he was entering her gently. Their lovemaking took on a satisfying and lengthy amount of time. Eventually, they drifted off asleep, still with their arms entwined.

The next day, they had breakfast in bed and took their time dressing.

They knew it was the end of a vacation, and it was back to work for both of them. She admitted that she was looking forward to seeing Lucky, even though she knew he probably hadn't thought about her. Mary kept him at her house for extended periods when she was gone, and he seemed to enjoy it with her and Winston. At least they haven't gotten into a fight yet.

Their next trip would be to Asheville with Roger and Mary. Ally was looking forward to that trip, seeing Billy Graham's home and museum and visiting the Biltmore House. She wanted to explore more of North Carolina. She and Mary will have to decide what to do with the animals. There was a lovely place where Mary took Winston to be groomed, and Mary said they would board overnight. So that was something to check out when she returned.

Before she left Bartow, Ally checked with her sister and was told their parent's sixtieth wedding anniversary was the following year, so they had time to plan. She was glad to know that; she hoped her father's dementia wouldn't progress further. Their anniversary wasn't until the fall, sometime in October. Now, she had something to look forward to next year. She and her sister would do the planning. Craig would help with the cost, but this required a feminine touch. She made a mental note to add it to her calendar so she would remember to ask Gene for the time off. Also, Neal would have to plan out his schedule. She couldn't wait until he retired.

chapter
19

S heriff Taylor and Agent Jay Camp, along with the FBI, arrived
unannounced at Jeffrey Edward's home at eleven a.m. Using
their credentials, they had to get past the neighborhood security.
When they arrived, they noted a three-car garage and no cars outside.

Mrs. Edwards opened the door and invited them in; after intro-
ductions, she directed them back to the sunroom. She called Jeffrey
upstairs, and he came down a few minutes later.

Sheriff Taylor introduced himself and Agent Camp to Mr. Edwards,
having already met Mrs. Edwards. Kellum noticed Mr. Edwards's height
and asked if he played basketball in college.

"No, I never played in college, but I did play some in high school. I
get that question a lot."

Agent Camp asked him where he went to school, and he said,
"UPenn, The Wharton School, you know, the same place Trump went."

"Oh, yes."

Kellum got down to business. "I'm sure you are both wondering
why we are here."

Jeffrey nodded his affirmation. Kellum continued, "We are looking
for a thirteen-year-old girl abducted from the Victory Mall in Blaylock

County. It happened late Friday afternoon, so you can understand that we are pursuing every lead."

Surprised, Jeffrey asked, "What can I do to help?"

"We have a witness who heard a conversation on or near the property you own off of Hwy 408, and we wondered if we could access a road with a gate with a no-trespassing sign. It is vitally important we do so this morning. Would you go with us or give us a key to the gate?" Kellum asked.

"I don't have any problem with doing that. I'll do whatever you want."

Jeffrey looked at his wife and said, "Stella, do you mind if I ride down to the property we purchased and unlock the gate?"

"No, anything that will help find her. Go," said his wife.

"Great, let's go. We'll follow you, sir."

On the way, Kellum told Agent Camp, "I don't feel good about this couple. What did you think?"

"I think we need to check out this property, and depending on what we find, we will install monitors in their vehicles, listening devices in their house, and listening devices on their phones. We cannot do anything without probable cause, not yet."

Jay Camp called Eliza and told her where they were headed. "Was there anything yet on the videos?"

"No, nothing yet, but still reviewing. There are so many cars of the same description, and the original video was too grainy. Two officers are out looking for cameras along the route they probably took. The problem is the freeway is just outside of the mall exit, so it is doubtful they will find many. I have notified all of the motels along the same probable route. I hope they holed up at some seedy place until the coast was clear. That fits our playbook. I have another possible contact, but I will keep it close to the vest until it pans out."

They were approaching the road to turn off. Jeffrey had put on his blinker, and Kellum recognized the place they just passed as where Brent and Angela had been. When Jeffrey arrived at the gate, he got out of his car and unlocked it using his key. He opened the gate inward wide enough to let both cars through. They followed him down the road and finally came to a clearing that had a small dwelling. Jeffrey stopped his car and got out. Jay and Kellum did the same.

"Well, this is all that is here. I occasionally let business partners and customers use the area for hunting. This old shack was here when I bought it, so I just left some supplies there. We can go in and look," he started walking up the wooden steps, and Jay and Kellum followed. Kellum was taking pictures with his cell phone. Jeffrey didn't object to it or say anything about it. After they looked around and saw no evidence that anyone had been there for a while, Kellum thanked Jeffrey for his time and asked if there was another exit.

"No, you must turn around and go out the same way."

"Okay, Mr. Edwards, we thank you for your time," said Kellum, and Jay nodded and shook his hand.

"No problem. I'm always glad to help law enforcement. My wife and I hope you find the young lady soon."

They stepped onto the porch and started for their cars, then Jay said, "Mr. Edwards, may I ask you a question?"

"Certainly," said Jeffrey.

"How would a car and a truck get down this road without a gate key? Does anyone else have one?"

Kellum looked at Jay, then at Jeffrey, waiting for his answer.

Jeffrey stumbled over his words like he didn't know what to say.

"Now that I think about it, I believe I once gave my handyman a key so he could come and check on the property. I'm not sure if he gave it back. I'll check on that and let you know."

"See that you do," said Jay, then he opened the passenger door and got in. Kellum stood there stunned, but at that moment, he straightened up and got in on the driver's side.

"Whew, he didn't see that coming," Kellum told Jay.

"I knew he wouldn't; that's why I did it that way. It isn't a deal breaker since Angela heard the voices in a different location, but I'm just curious if anyone else knows about it."

Jeffrey turned around first, and Kellum followed him out. Once Kellum got on the highway, Jay called his boss and asked for the Edwards to be put under surveillance, 'the whole enchilada.' He told him about being at one of the properties where they had a witness who had overheard a conversation close to there. He also advised him there was a three-car garage at their home, and it was in a secure neighborhood. He said they found in searching the tax records that Edwards had an office in Raleigh, but he would get back to him with the address. "He is a hedge-fund manager, so he probably works out of his home, too."

His boss asked him why he was a suspect. "A feeling and the accessibility. He appeared to have the finer things. It's not a coincidence that the witnesses heard what they heard near his property. It looks like this could be a case of sex trafficking."

Kellum looked at him and said, "You don't mess around."

"This is nothing to mess around with."

He told Kellum that Eliza had an excellent reputation working on human trafficking cases. "She was called in for a reason. Ask her sometime how she got into that aspect of it. It will surprise you."

"Can't you tell me?"

"Sorry, but it's not my story to tell. Best left to her."

chapter

20

After Jeffrey secured the gate lock and was back in his car, he made his phone call. When the line was answered, he said, "Don't make any moves until you hear from me."

"Okay, boss. I may need additional sedatives; she still fights whenever she wakes up."

"I'll take care of it." Jeffrey had been using a Mexican pharmacy for sedatives for years. It was even easier now to get drugs, but he stuck with the same pharmacy because he knew he could trust them not to lace any Fentanyl in his shipment. That would be all he would need was to get in a fix with a Fentanyl overdose.

Jeffrey was nervous now. That FBI agent was suspicious. He knew that when he asked him about the extra key. He needed to think. The plan was falling apart. He next called his partner, Senator Clayton, but got his voicemail. He left an urgent message asking him to contact him. He sometimes felt he did all the work while they shared the profits. He may ditch Britt and start taking all the profits, but the thought just occurred to him: if he goes down, so does the good Senator. That thought pleased him.

When he got home, Stella was getting ready to go shopping. He needed to go to the office and get some work done. His day was almost shot. He planned a business dinner that night but decided to cancel it. The client wasn't among his top one hundred, so he wasn't worried about hurting his feelings. Most of his work was wining and dining clients. It could be so monotonous at times. Stella would be disappointed, but she would have to get over it. He called his assistant and had her make the call to cancel the dinner, saying he had a conflict and would reschedule later. He had heard from another 'client' he would rather see.

After their conversation, he called Walter, who he knew had the key to the property, and told him he had been overheard discussing the abduction.

"Really? Sorry, boss. I had no idea. Is it going to change anything?"

"I don't know yet. I am rearranging her pickup time. We need to lay low for a while because I have the heat on me now. Whatever you do, please don't lose that key, don't tell anyone you have it, and, for crying out loud, don't get picked up for any reason. How is your eye?"

"It's okay, boss. I'm just sore, and it doesn't look infected."

"That's good. Vinnie's with you?"

"Yes, sir. He is, and he goes out to get our food. I was afraid to go out with my eye bandaged. We are okay."

"Okay, hang tight until you hear from me. Meeting up may take a few days; be patient, you will get paid."

Jeffrey started working on some of his clients' accounts when he got to his office. He had to admit he had his mind on other things lately and needed to pay more attention to some of his work. As far as he knew, the market had been on a roll, and his clients were happy. His assistant had opened his mail and stacked it in order of importance. She had been with him for many years, and he trusted her with personal and private matters. He had helped her children and grandchildren with tuition, and she was very loyal to him for it.

He worked through the multitude of mail, primarily solicitations for money. He and his wife were generous with charitable contributions, so he took her the ones he liked and let her decide. However, his email was private, and only he had the password. He had it locked down with so much security that Fort Knox would be envious. He enjoyed his privacy regarding his women, especially the porn sites he frequented.

Stella would never know about this part of his life unless he died before her, and then she might find out about it. He was against child pornography and found anyone who engaged in it sick.

He came by it, honestly. Unfortunately for him, he found an uncle staying with his parents when he was around six who was looking at magazines of child pornography. He almost told his parents, but his uncle caught him looking at him masturbating and figured out Jeffrey knew about the magazines. He went into his room that night and threatened that if he ever mentioned it to anyone, he would find out exactly what it was all about.

Of course, Jeffrey realized years later that it was only a threat because his uncle would have gone to prison if he had told on him. Jeffrey didn't know then that he was just out of jail for the attempted rape of a six-year-old girl. There had been very little evidence, so he got a light sentence, and his family connections didn't hurt. He avoided being near his uncle again, and a few months later, his uncle committed suicide. Jeffrey asked his parents why, but they never gave him a good answer. He learned years later from an aunt that Clark had raped a ten-year-old girl and knew he was going to prison. He knew why they had sex offender laws and agreed with them. Consensual sex was one thing, but rape, particularly of a child, was another.

While daydreaming, he was jolted back to reality when his assistant buzzed him and said Ms. Kennedy was there for her appointment.

"Send her in," Jeffrey said. He got up, greeted Katarina at the door, and locked it behind her. Jeffrey thought she looked ravishing with her beautiful ash-blonde hair and piercing blue eyes. He wrapped his arm around her waist and nuzzled her neck. "You don't know how much I have missed you," he said.

"And I you," purred Katarina. She removed her new Stuart Weitzman heels, walked to the sofa, and sat down. Her red dress had a slit that showed off her beautiful left thigh. Jeffrey poured each of them a whiskey, took one over to her, got on his knee, and started rubbing her leg until he reached her underwear. From there, he had easy access to her sweet spot. She threw her head back and said, "Take me. I am ready."

Jeffrey had already removed his shirt and tie. He still had a good physique, even at his age. He noticed a few graying hairs on his chest, but Katarina had never complained. He was at least twice her age. He removed his trousers and his underwear. All that was left was his socks. With those, he didn't bother. He located the condoms he kept in a special drawer on his side table. By then, Katarina was wearing her red lace bra and underwear. He gently removed her underwear, climbed on top of her, and entered her gently. Her purrs were so soft as not to alert his assistant. That was how it went for several minutes as he reached a final climax. Katarina was also spent. Her face seemed to get flushed when they made love. Jeffrey kissed her breast, then her mouth, and thanked her for an enjoyable afternoon.

"So formal," Katarina whispered. She hoped to catch him off guard, and maybe he would slip up and give her some information she could relay to Eliza. He seemed in a hurry when she first came in, and the lovemaking was more rushed than usual.

She rolled off the sofa and went into the bathroom to freshen up and redress. When she finished, she came out and kissed him gently on the lips, using her tongue to enter his mouth, and pressed her breasts to his chest. She purred, "Call me."

The visit didn't yield anything useful except an enjoyable climax. She wished she could have gotten something for Eliza but knew Jeffrey would call on her again soon. He had never visited her apartment as long as she had become his paramour. He paid for it and gave her the money to furnish it. In a way, she was glad he hadn't been there. A girl needed something for herself. She still worked at the strip club, but it was getting old. She knew she would like to retire from freelance sex work, but what else would she do? She still had her looks, and her figure was something that turned heads.

She liked being an FBI informant and had helped in several sting operations. They were not pleasant; they often required oral sex, and when she participated, it caused her to remember the horrors of growing up in Russia. No, she would stay as an FBI informant because she knew they would take care of her. New York was so beautiful in December. That was the only time she went there.

chapter

21

Agent Camp called Eliza and said, "The unit is ready to start the surveillance. They were watching the home, and they knew that neither was home.

"The problem was they have a security system. They knew he was at work, and they had put a tracer on his car. I don't think the wife is involved, so that we can hold off on her car for now. I didn't get the vibe off of her that I did off of him. He owes me an answer to my question about the key, so I will go to his house this evening with that question and make up a few more.

"Why don't you come with me and keep them engaged? I can put the listening device somewhere. You know the old trick of asking to use the bathroom? Capeesh?"

"Capeesh. What time? How about eight? They both should be home by then," said Eliza.

"I'll call as we are close and tell him we are in the neighborhood and have more questions. I'll make it sound casual. I don't want him to know we suspect him."

"Great. That'll work," said Eliza.

"Also, I need to tell you that I mentioned to Sheriff Taylor that you have an interesting story about why you got into human trafficking. He may ask you one of these days. Hope you're not upset with me," said Jay

"That's fine. I'm not upset with you."

Eliza was at the station and overseeing some of the videos. There were a couple of promising ones, and she had sent the deputies out to see if they could find witnesses. Meanwhile, she planned to go to each of the friend's houses today and try to do a more extensive interview.

She's reviewed their initial interviews from the afternoon it happened but wanted to see if they remembered anything else. The initial shock should have worn off by now, and she hoped they would think of something else. But before that, she went by Williams's home and interviewed Mrs. Williams.

On her way over, she thought about her discussion with Katarina this morning. Katarina was an FBI informant recruited in New York City five years ago. She was a prostitute, but she preferred to call herself an escort. Eliza met her when she was going through the academy. Eliza had Russian relatives now living in the States, so they had that in common. At the time, Katarina had just started as an informant. The handler onboarded her after her third arrest. The officer who arrested her felt sorry for her because he knew she had no family, no one that cared about her. He got her a day pass that year as a favor from the judge to take her to his home for Christmas.

His daughters were only five and seven. They were fascinated by her accent and her beauty. His wife very graciously taught her how to cook the Christmas turkey. They made several other dishes that Katarina had never heard of, much less ever tasted. She fell in love with cranberry sauce. She was fascinated that you can also buy it in a can. She said she would buy every can on the shelf when she could. Of course, the officer knew it would be a while before she could do that.

After that day, he went to the judge and suggested that with Katarina's skills, perhaps she could help with the Russian mob problem in New York. The judge told him he had a contact with the FBI and would get in touch with him.

It took about six months, but the FBI called Katarina and set her up to become an informant. She had been doing it ever since. She continued celebrating Christmas with the officer and his family. He was now a detective with the NYPD; his children were almost teenagers. Katarina bought them all gifts just like they were her family. She also brought the cranberry sauce every year.

Eliza reached out to her this morning, and they had a great talk. She knew Katarina had been sent to the Raleigh area and was also on the task force to detect and find child traffickers. She told Eliza it was rewarding but so deplorable. "I don't think some of them will ever be recovered."

After Eliza told her what she was working on and why she was calling, Katarina told her she was lucky. "I have been trying to bring that bastard in for about two years. We knew he was involved in human trafficking but never children. I owe him an afternoon visit, so I will call him to see if he needs some fun. I can put a recorder in one of my shoes; he will never suspect. They are so beautiful and expensive but so worth it. The best thing I've ever gotten out of doing this job," she laughed.

"Perfect. Good luck and be safe. You have my number, so call me later if you have anything to report," said Eliza.

Eliza arrived at the Williams home at two o'clock. Mrs. Williams was in the sunroom, and one of her friends opened the door and took her back there. "Hello, Mrs. Williams. I am Eliza Mancini. I arrived the day after Lisa disappeared. We are doing everything we can to help get Lisa home."

"Please call me Michelle, and yes, I know the FBI and Sheriff Taylor and his deputies are working very hard. I am praying all day and night that she will be home soon; do you believe in God, Agent Mancini?"

Eliza was surprised at the question but answered honestly, "Yes, I do. I assure you of that, and your prayers will be answered. I have a few questions, if I may. She looked at the friend, and Michelle noticed it and said, "This is my best friend, and I want her to stay, please."

"No problem. Michelle, had Lisa been threatened or afraid in any way in the days before her abduction? Are there any unusual cars up and down your street? Was she seeing anyone at the time?"

"She was only thirteen, so no, she was not seeing anyone. We didn't want her to start dating until she was sixteen. That was how old her sister, Linda, was before she could date, and it was never an issue. As far as if there was a strange car, I don't know. There are so many cars on the road; how would I know if there was a strange one?

"She never mentioned being threatened or afraid. I must tell you, though, Lisa was a lot to handle. I thought she would be the death of me."

"What do you mean?" asked Eliza.

"She was back-talking, not doing chores. She frankly was a brat. I'm sorry to say that, and I hope I get to hold that brat again, but that was exactly what she was."

Eliza noted she looked at her friend, who nodded in agreement. "I don't want to upset you anymore, Michelle, but please tell me, out of all her friends, who was her best friend? Or BFF, like the young girls say these days."

"That's easy. It was Tiffany. Tiffany Armano. They were inseparable."

"Thank you. You have been a big help. I pray for you and your family every night."

chapter

22

Jeffrey arrived home around five. Stella was still out but left him a note saying she would return by six. Since they were not going out with his client, she would pick up Chinese at their favorite restaurant. She left a heart sign after her name.

He went upstairs and took a shower. He wanted to get the smell of sex off of him before she got home. His suit was put in a bag for dry cleaning and would be taken to the cleaners tomorrow morning. He heard the garage door go up and knew Stella was here already, so he turned the shower on full blast to drown her out and took a most pleasurable shower. Afterward, he put on his casual docksiders and Greg Norman shirt. He came downstairs looking rested and clean. He gave her a big kiss and patted her rear end. She reacted for a change, glanced over her shoulder, and winked.

After they ate the Chinese dinner, Jeffrey cleaned the kitchen while she went up and showered. She wore a black casual sleeveless long dress and sandals when she came down. She had put her hair in a clasp at the nape of her neck. They went out on the sunporch, and she picked up the latest Donna Picerno book, and he turned on the Braves game. They thought they were in for the night, but then his phone rang, and it was Jay Camp, the FBI agent he met earlier.

"I'm in your area running down some leads and wondered if I could stop by for just a few minutes. I have Agent Mancini, whom I don't think you have met yet. Would it be okay?"

Caught off guard, he looked over at Stella and said, "Sure, we were just relaxing. How long before you will be here?"

"About ten minutes." Jay wanted to give him enough time to gather his thoughts while also making him a little unnerved. It was a tactic he had used many times.

As promised, about ten minutes later, the doorbell rang. Jeffrey hopped up to answer it and invited them both in. Jay introduced Agent Mancini to Jeffrey and again to his wife in the sunroom.

"I smell Chinese," said Eliza. "I hope we aren't disturbing dinner."

"No, we were done," answered Stella. She remained in her comfortable seat and kept her book in her lap.

"Well, for one thing," Jay started, "I was wondering about the extra key?"

Before Jeffrey could answer, Jay asked if he could use the restroom.

"Of course, down the hall and to your right and at the end of that hall."

When Jay returned, Jeffrey said, "I checked with my handyman, Walter, who had not returned it and apologized. He promised to drop it off this week."

Eliza noted that Stella looked up with no expression and looked at Jeffrey. This tell made her more curious about what Stella knew.

"Great, please give me his phone number and address if you have it. I want to follow up with him to see if he was one of the people there that night when Angela heard the voices."

Eliza again noted Stella was listening to this conversation and not reading the book but didn't say anything.

Jeffrey stumbled for a second with his words again and pulled his phone out of his pocket. Jay wrote down the number as Jeffrey read it off to him. He thanked Jeffrey and Stella for their time and for allowing him to use the bathroom.

"My wife wants me to drink eight glasses of water daily, and you never know when you need to go. It can be inconvenient," he chuckled.

Eliza thought his timing was perfect. He doesn't think Jeffrey or his wife suspected Jay was doing anything besides using the bathroom.

"Was there anything else you needed?" asked Jeffrey.

"Yes, please, we need you to account for your whereabouts that night?" asked Eliza.

Jeffrey was busy pulling up his calendar on his phone, "Remind me again the date, please."

"June 21, a Tuesday."

"That's easy; I play poker at the club every Tuesday night. You can check on that by stopping by there. It's the Windsor Country Club on the Eastside." He looked over at Stella and smiled as he said this, Eliza noted.

"Okay, that was all we needed. I hope we didn't impose too much on your evening. We can see our way out."

Eliza and Jay nodded at Stella Edwards, and Jay shook Jeffrey's hand.

Once in the car, Eliza looked at Jay, and he looked at her, and both said, "He's involved."

"When I went to the bathroom, I put a microphone inside a lampshade on a table in the hallway. I don't think he will say anything in front of his wife, but you never know. I didn't see a landline. The cars were in the garage, so I would have to try to follow her to get a locator on her vehicle.

"That may be more difficult. She probably doesn't have set times to come and go. I don't think she was in on this. She looked up several times when we were talking with her husband. I think she was as curious as we were," said Eliza.

Before returning to Murray, they found a Cookout and enjoyed burgers and drinks. They sat in the parking lot and analyzed what they had.

Eliza said, "We know his handyman was on the property, and I believe it was him that Angela heard. I know Mr. Edwards is unfaithful to his wife, and I will go ahead and tell you how I know that. I am telling you about an informant, so there are no names; you may want to use her one day. She had been in this area for about two years and met Jeffrey at a gentleman's club in town during a lunch hour. She originally met him in NYC a few years ago. He remembered her when he saw her in the club; she's been exclusive to him since then. She told me she would see him today and put a listening device in her shoe in case he says anything. She sees him for sex, so you will hear the usual sounds, nothing you haven't heard before, yes?"

"Yes," agreed Jay.

"Well, if she was successful, she will call me later tonight."

"Okay, I don't have nearly as much. What if I run out tomorrow and take a technician to dust around the lock for fingerprints? It might be helpful. While at it, I could take a magnetic sensor to look for bullet casings. We need to get some drones over that area and call in the K9 unit if we find anything. A few leads were coming in; a few were from the Amber Alert, but they didn't have enough information. Whoever planned this caper covered their tracks pretty well," Jay concluded.

"First thing in the morning, I will call this phone number he gave us. He may have given me a fake number, but I don't want to deal with it tonight. Let him stew in his juices overnight. Then, I will visit Lisa's BFF, Miss Tiffany Armano. Probably Italian, like me, huh?" asked Eliza, rhetorically.

Jay said, "I'll go to the country club he mentioned and check his alibi for that night."

After the FBI agents left, Stella asked Jeffrey what that was all about.

"They were following up on something one of Lisa's friends thought she overheard. It couldn't be anything important. Walter was probably out at the property and may have had one of his friends with him. I don't think Walter could find his way out of a wet paper bag, much less get involved in a kidnapping," he laughed.

Stella said nothing but stored the conversation in her head for future purposes. She didn't always believe what her husband told her.

chapter

23

Gene was concerned about his cousin, Trent, and wondered if they had found Lisa. He had been unable to see the news because he had been so busy at work. He checked his phone for news and found the original report, but nothing was updated. He could call Eliza but didn't want to compromise her because she could be in the middle of something more important. Sara knew something was on his mind because he had just walked in and gone straight to his office. She had several messages for him that had just arrived this morning.

She knocked on his door, and he said, "Come in." She stepped into his office, and he looked up and said, "I'm sorry I didn't say hello."

"No worries. I thought you had something on your mind. Is there anything I can do to help?" Sara asked.

"No, I just have a family matter and will need to call my new cousin, at least new to me," he chuckled.

He hesitated to tell Sara that the girl who was abducted was related to him. He was concerned about slipping up, and she may have realized that was why Eliza wasn't working now. Once he learned Eliza's real reason for working for him, he had been walking on eggshells. Lately, he wished he didn't know.

"Eliza called and wanted you to call her. Also, we had an inquiry for next Saturday and another for the Friday and Saturday after that.

"Should I send them the standard proposals and find out what they would like?"

"Sure, that will work. If they have any special requests, run them by me. Have you had any responses to our want ad yet?"

"Yes, that was another thing I wanted to tell you. I had three calls late yesterday since the paper came out that day, and all three sounded interested in an interview. One said they had experience. They all sounded like college-aged kids—two males and one female. Should I set up appointments?"

"Yes, check my calendar, and let's try to get them in here soon. Finding good people was getting harder and harder, so we needed to get something going; Eliza being out on personal leave is leaving us a huge hole. I think Ally will pick some jobs up since she's back now," said Gene.

He worked on some menu ideas for the next hour. He had been watching some cooking shows and finding more exciting appetizers. His clients seemed to be more interested in what the appetizers were than the entrees. He believes the trend was because people are getting more into wines and like having time to unwind before meals with a couple of glasses. He was happy to do whatever the client wanted but knew he needed to stay competitive to maintain a growing clientele.

His clients leaned more high-end and seemed to appreciate his eye for detail. Of course, Sara was a big part of that. Her customer service skills improved; his wait staff helped because they seemed more refined. He was a stickler about his wait staff's wardrobe. He told them no flashy jewelry. All of that allowed him to attract and keep customers.

He had waited to call Eliza until after nine out of courtesy, but now it was a quarter after, so he called her cell phone. She picked up on the first ring, "Good morning."

"How are you, and more importantly, have you completed your task?"

"Not yet, but several leads have developed, and I am working furiously to check on them. I think we have a shot. You're probably wondering when I will be back?"

"That too, although I hated to bring it up."

"I would guesstimate another two weeks, hopefully less. I always need some time to decompress."

"Understood, just find her, please," said Gene.

"Yes, sir." She hung up.

Eliza pulled out her notebook and found Tiffany Armano's address and telephone number. She called ahead as a courtesy and spoke with her mother. She agreed it would be okay for her to see Tiffany this morning. She then called the phone number Mr. Edwards provided for his handyman. His name was Walter Green. He answered on the third ring and sounded out of breath.

"Good morning. This is Agent Eliza Mancini. I am working on the missing thirteen-year-old girl's case and have some questions. Do you have time?"

"Sure, Mr. Edwards called and told me you might be calling," he told her.

Great, thought, Eliza. *Edwards called him so they could get their story straight, and this guy was dumb enough to tell me.* She rolled her eyes.

"Were you on Supe's Creek Rd on June 21st?" she decided to get right to the point and maybe catch him off guard.

"I was there that day, and after talking to Mr. Edwards, I realized that I had left the key in my truck's glove compartment," said Walter.

"Well, these things do happen. Where is the key now?"

"It is still in the truck, as far as I know. Do you want me to bring it to you?"

"That won't be necessary. Where were you on the night of Tuesday, June 21st?"

"I would have been at home with my wife, probably watching a baseball game," said Walter.

"Okay, that's all for now. Thank you for your time."

"I hope I have been of some help," said Walter.

Yeah, right, thought Eliza.

On her way to the Armano's, she passed the station and picked up Agent Camp. She told him about the call to Walter Green this morning: "He claims he was at home that night with his wife, probably watching a baseball game, but he copped to being on Supe's Creek during the day. He told me the key was still in his truck's glove compartment and offered to bring it to me. I told him no."

"He sounds eager to help, huh?"

"Yeah, right."

"I went to the country club this morning and spoke with the bartender, and he verified they have a poker game every Tuesday night. Mr. Edwards was a regular, but could not confirm whether he was there that night. He told me to call Mr. Edwards for a contact to confirm, and when I called Jeffrey, he gave me Senator Britt Clayton's name and number. I called Senator Clayton, who was happy to confirm his playing on the 21st; he even pulled up his calendar to verify it for me. Convenient, huh?"

chapter

24

S ara reached two of the three who had inquired about the job. After seeing Gene's calendar was clear, she scheduled them for one and two o'clock that afternoon. She knew one of them. He was the son of one of her neighbors, and she thought he was a friendly, polite kid. She understood from his mother that he was enrolled in the local college and was taking culinary classes.

"I made you two appointments for today," Sara told Gene after making sure he was not on a call in his office.

"Great. What times?"

"The first is at one o'clock and the other at two. I figured back to back, and you could get them out of the way. By the way, I can vouch for the first one because he's the son of a neighbor of mine. He's taking culinary classes at the local college."

"His name is Lonnie Vickers. The other is a little older, and her name is Annie Mason. I already checked out their references, and they were good. Annie had a solid work record at a restaurant in Myrtle Beach. She told me she recently relocated due to her husband's job transfer. He's with a construction company here in Brunswick County."

"Well, there is certainly enough construction going on in this county. Traffic is getting worse and worse."

"Boy, are you right!" she exclaimed.

Gene was impressed with how well Sara had transitioned into the office manager role. She worked hard and was beginning to be his right-hand man, so to speak. He made a mental note to check what he was paying her. It may be time to review her pay and make her a salaried employee. It was an idea he had been considering for a while. His business was growing fast. Soon, he would have to consider getting another catering kitchen. He had been turning away business due to insufficient capacity to handle it all. He and Sara had discussed what a good problem he had, but he had not made a plan to do anything about it. He knew he would have to expand, and it was time to find a solution.

The COVID pandemic had caused them to struggle a bit, and he had cut back on his salary and benefits to accommodate keeping them afloat. He was so glad Ally came along when she did. She had proved to be a flexible employee and an essential part of his team. She helped Sara out when she needed it. Ally had a good head on her shoulders, and he couldn't imagine not having her. She had been with him for two years, and as far as he knew, she hadn't had a raise or complained about it. It was time he started giving end-of-the-year bonuses. He made another note to check into how to go about doing that. He knew he needed to contact his accountant, Andrews and Associates, to see if he could afford to increase salaries and give bonuses.

He called his accountant and made an appointment for the day after tomorrow. *Good*, he thought. *At least I took care of one goal.* Now, he was looking forward to meeting the two interviewees today. He went on Facebook Market Place to see if he could locate another catering kitchen. He found two: one was in Alabama, a little too far away, but the other was in South Carolina, a little town called Walterboro. He read the description, and it sounded like something he could use. It wasn't too old, but he didn't know the story behind it...there was always a story.

He went ahead and messaged the person and asked if they could give him more information, like why they were selling. The price wasn't too bad, so he was anxious to hear from them.

It was close to twelve-thirty now, and he was getting hungry. He had an engagement tonight and had to leave by four o'clock, so he wanted to make sure he had a good lunch beforehand. He told Sara he would run to the Waffle House up the street to get lunch. "Do you want me to bring you anything?"

"No, I'm good. I brought a salad from home, but thanks."

"Okay, I'll be back by one for the interview."

At the Waffle House, he ordered their special: an open-faced roast beef sandwich and a small salad. Sara mentioned a salad, which made him remember that he needed to eat more greens. The waitress's name was Lynn; he had known her for a long time, at least since moving here. She was a lovely redhead who never seemed to age. He knew she was divorced because she had mentioned her 'ex' several times. They appeared to be on good terms.

She had a daughter who'd started at UNCW. He couldn't believe it had been that long. He remembered her in first grade and thought, *how time flies*. He wondered if Lynn had a boyfriend because he would like to ask her out. It had been quite a while since he had dated anyone. His entire life was spent working.

"How are you doing, Lynn?"

"Oh, you know, about the same. I need a plumber. Do you know any good ones?"

"I might. What do you need to be done?"

"I have a leaky faucet, something simple, I think, but I wouldn't know where to start."

"If it is simple, I could do it for you," he told her confidently.

"Really? That would be great."

"Would this Saturday morning be soon enough, or are you working?" he asked her.

"Saturday is fine. I got stuck with the Sunday shift this weekend."

"Okay, give me your address, and I'll be there by nine. Just have a hot cup of coffee for me."

Gene returned to the office in time to see his first interviewee arrive as he was entering. As he walked past, he told Sara to bring him back.

When Lonnie came into his office, Gene stood and shook his hand. "Please have a seat and tell me a little about yourself."

"I'm enrolled at the local college and am taking culinary classes, sir."

"That's great. I understand you're a neighbor of my assistant, Sara. She spoke very highly of you," said Gene, trying to put him at ease.

They talked a bit more, and the subject eventually became sports teams. "I understand the college has quite a good baseball team," said Gene.

"Yes, as a matter of fact, they do," Lonnie affirmed.

"Well, if you are interested in the job, we could use you. Sara has already checked your references, and I trust her judgment."

"I am interested and am ready to start," said Lonnie.

"I'll have you finish some paperwork with Sara, and we will pair you up with another assistant. It will probably be Ally. Sara will let you know the dress code and what to expect. Can you work this weekend?" asked Gene.

"Yes, sir."

The next candidate arrived on time, and Gene liked her immediately. She was professional and well-spoken. He had Sara finish her paperwork and review the schedule. He told Sara to alternate their schedules for now, which she already knew to do. She would pair each of them with Ally because she knew Ally would be a great instructor.

chapter

25

Eliza and Agent Camp arrived at the Armano's home by ten. Eliza noted that it was a two-story brick home with a circular driveway. She was impressed with the beautiful rose garden in the front yard and commented on it when Mrs. Armano greeted them at the door.

"Yes, my mother loved roses, and she gave me a rose bush when each of my children was born. I kept adding to it for occasions like Mother's Day. I don't have a green thumb, but they do well in that spot. The problem, of course, is that the deer love them, so I keep them sprayed with a deterrent. It's supposed to be non-toxic, and it seems to keep them away."

They entered the living room, where Tiffany was already waiting. They sat in the chairs where Mrs. Armano directed them while she sat with Tiffany on the sofa across from them.

Eliza formally introduced herself and Agent Camp to Tiffany and her mother. She noted Tiffany was visibly shaking, and she wondered why.

"Tiffany, Agent Camp, and I are searching for Lisa with the help of Sheriff Taylor and the police force. We are reinterviewing her friends, particularly those with her, the day she disappeared. We need to know if you remember anything about that afternoon or anything in the previous days that could help us."

"I don't know anything else," Tiffany replied with tears in her eyes. Her mom looked at her and said, "Tiffany, please help the agents if you know anything. They need your cooperation."

Eliza wondered why her mother put it that way and suspected Tiffany knew more than she claimed.

"Tiffany, you are not in trouble. Neither are your friends. You didn't know what would happen, so if you are holding back anything, please tell us now. It could be the difference in finding Lisa or not."

Tiffany nodded but kept quiet.

Eliza still noted Tiffany's discomfort and wondered if it was because she didn't want to say more in front of her mother. She decided to try another approach. "Mrs. Armano, would you mind if we interview Tiffany alone?"

Mrs. Armano seemed to get the message Eliza was conveying and said, "Of course, I will be upstairs if you need me." She squeezed Tiffany's hand when she stood to walk out.

Tiffany watched her mother go, then turned to the agents and said, "I'm sorry. I didn't want to bring this up in front of my mother, but Lisa had a boyfriend. Well, actually, many boyfriends. She spent the night with me just a couple of nights before the abduction, I think that previous Tuesday, and sneaked out with her latest boyfriend.

"She told me the next day that a car was parked near them and flashed its lights toward them as they slowly pulled away. She said it was a dark car, but they did not know what kind. It spooked them both, and she felt she needed to tell me. Now I wonder if they were watching her," then she added, "Lisa had sex with her boyfriends," she looked only at Eliza when she told them this tidbit.

Not missing a beat, Agent Camp asked for the name and number of the boyfriend she was with that night. Tiffany was still showing her obvious distress but went and got her cell phone from the kitchen, brought it back, and gave him the name Stewart Mankiewicz, along with his phone number.

"Thank you," said Eliza. "Anything else you can think of?"

Tiffany shook her head and told them no. Eliza still thought she knew more but decided not to push her right now. They stood up, thanked her, and asked her to thank her mother for them. Eliza gave her card to Tiffany and told her to call her anytime, day or night if she remembered anything else. Tiffany looked up at her and nodded, still with tears in her big brown eyes.

In the car, Eliza told Jay, "I think she may know more but was afraid of her mother or of getting Lisa in more trouble. Do you think this could be a teenage stunt?"

"No, I didn't get that vibe. I think she was sincerely worried about her friend. Hey, we have more than we had before. Let's get back to the station and tell the Sheriff. He may know this, Mankiewicz kid."

Sheriff Taylor was in his office reviewing tips when they walked in. He asked Eliza and Jay, "Do you know how many kooks are in the world?"

"Yeah, we have a pretty good idea," said Eliza. "We have a possible lead from talking with Tiffany. Do you know Stewart Mankiewicz?"

"I do. He is a high school football player. What does he have to do with this?" asked Kellum.

"He and Lisa were out together doing what teenagers do, but a little more, if you get the drift, unbeknownst to her parents or Tiffany's. She sneaked out to be with him on Tuesday before she disappeared, and they had sex. A car shined its lights on the car they were in and left them on it long enough for them both to feel uncomfortable. Lisa told Tiffany about it the next day. She was shaken up and visibly upset about it. Tiffany now wonders if they were stalking Lisa."

"She didn't mention that when I interviewed her at the mall. I guess she was still in shock. I know where the place is, I think. We sometimes ride through there to give them a little jolt, but I don't think we have been there recently. Did she say if they recognized the car?"

"No, she told her they saw a dark car and couldn't see who was in it or what kind it was because of the lights. It sounds kind of like what Angela saw."

"I think it is time for you to interview Mankiewicz. He is only sixteen, so he may ask to bring a parent, but he will probably come alone under the circumstances," said Kellum.

"I agree, but since we only collect information, cooperating fully would be in his best interest. It's going to be here or at his house. We will give him the choice," said Jay.

"I agree," said Eliza.

Agent Camp reached for his phone and dialed Stewart's number. He answered immediately. Jay explained why he was calling and asked him to come to the station. He agreed and said he would be there shortly.

Stewart knew he was going to get a call. It was inevitable. One of his buddies told him to expect a call. He wondered who told the police about him and Lisa. He didn't think it would be Brent. He always seemed like a straight-up guy who wouldn't rat out anyone even if he knew. *But if my sister were missing, I would probably do the same,* he thought.

chapter

26

Lisa was becoming delirious due to her condition. She hadn't eaten in almost two days and barely drank the water they kept shoving at her. Her mind was playing tricks on her. She noticed they wore masks when they came in to check on her. She was blindfolded whenever they moved her, which had not been since last night. She heard voices from another part of the house. It wasn't audible enough for her to understand what they were saying.

She cried for her mother and father. She felt broken and hated that she had been such a horrible person. Although she didn't attend church regularly, she believed in God and prayed for redemption and salvation. Her parents took them when they were little, but it all stopped when she became a teenager. She chose not to be with the nerdy kids that did go to church.

She wanted to be with the cool kids who liked drinking and smoking weed. She realized she didn't like doing it much but went along just to be cool.

She now wished she had not started having sex at such a young age. She wondered if she was kidnapped for sex trafficking rather than a ransom.

These thoughts kept going through her mind, and she was about to go crazy. She was sure her parents were worried and beside themselves. Her brother, Brent, was such a good guy. He was probably looking for her, too. His girlfriend, Angela, was not in with the cool kids, which sounded good to her now. She knew Angela was poor but didn't seem ashamed of her circumstances. That's probably why Brent was so into her. Angela was a good person and wished she was more like her. If and when she ever got out of this mess, she promised to straighten up and become a better person, which included no sex and going to church.

She hoped her sister would come home to be with their mother and give her support. Linda was a rock star in high school, always had good grades, participated in sports, and was in various clubs. She was a bit of a nerd but was popular. She was doing great at college; she prayed her predicament wasn't ruining Linda's life, too.

Oops, now someone was entering the room. They had at least three locks to undo to open the door. The room was darkened with sheets over the windows, but they kept the overhead light on. She supposed they didn't want her to look out. She had been listening for cars, trucks, or anything to give her a hint of where she was; she knew she was still close to her home because neither trip seemed longer than an hour. At least, she thought that was the case. She had been drugged most of that time, though.

"Here is some food. I hope you will eat. Do you need to get up to the potty chair?" asked the woman.

"No and no," said Lisa.

"I am going to leave it here on a stool. You can reach it with your free arm. You need to eat something. It is a chicken sandwich. Here is another bottle of water. I've loosened the top for you. I will be back in half an hour."

Lisa didn't react. She waited for the woman to leave. She smelled the food, and her stomach was growling so bad she decided to eat it. With some difficulty, she reached over and grabbed it with her right arm. It was so good. She drank all of the water, too. The next time the woman showed up, she would ask to use the bedside potty, which was disgusting, but she would need to go eventually.

Since she had quit kicking at them, they no longer medicated her. She felt like she was coming out of her fog of drugs. She never realized what these drugs could do. Weed was one thing; she would get a little high, but she never tried anything more serious, and now she knew she never would. She knew who the drug dealers were at school. There was a severe heroin problem festering amongst the older kids; the drugs were so affordable and accessible to get. She thought about whether she would get out of this mess. That was the second time she had said, 'If I get out of this mess.' She knew she must start thinking more positively and ensure she left alive and well. She decided to engage the woman in conversation the next time she came in to see if she would tell her what she knew. She thought she couldn't be too bright if she got hooked up with these losers, so maybe she would let something slip.

The woman came back when she said she would and was pleased to see that Lisa had eaten the sandwich. "Would you please help me to the bathroom?" asked Lisa.

The woman looked surprised when Lisa politely asked, "Yes, I will be happy to." She pulled her key out and unlocked the ankle bracelet. Lisa did most of the work and sat down on the bedside potty. After she had completed her business, she told the woman who had her back turned that she was through. The woman gave her the toilet paper roll, which they kept out of her reach, and she finished up. Lisa stood, turned, and got back in bed.

"May I ask you a question?" asked Lisa.

"Yes, what is it?"

"Would you tell me where we are and why I am here?" asked Lisa.

"You know I won't do that, so don't try to get it out of me." She turned to leave but remembered to get the bucket to dispose of its contents and clean it.

"Okay, could I just get something to stimulate me, like a crossword puzzle, a book, anything?" she looked at the woman pleadingly.

"I'll see what I can do." She left and made sure she secured all of the locks on the door.

Lisa lay back on the pillows, shut her eyes, and tried remembering her bedroom and house. Then, she began remembering Christmas mornings. She thought of Hannah, her favorite doll. That seemed to cheer her up and get her through the next few hours. She finally succumbed to sleep.

chapter

27

Stewart was rattled when he got the call from Agent Camp. He was worried about Lisa, and so was everyone he knew. He helped Tiffany by putting up posters around town. He visited Lisa's house and talked with her brother, Brent.

Brent was a great guy, and he was hurting. His mom was a total wreck. He didn't ask to see her when he was at the house, but he knew from others that she was on the brink of a breakdown. Lisa's father was still going to work, but he figured it was only because he had so much responsibility since he was co-owner. One of his friends who worked there told him Mr. Williams looked stressed. He was letting his brother take care of most of the business. Lisa's disappearance had been all everyone was talking about.

He planned to attend the vigil tomorrow night at the high school. His parents wanted to go with him, which he thought was nice. Tiffany and her friends planned and organized it.

Stewart arrived at the station just before one o'clock. Agent Camp led him into the small interrogation room. Collectively, they all decided he would be the one to question Stewart first, man to man. If he got any vibe that Stewart wasn't being forthright, he would have Sheriff Taylor intercede.

"Have a seat, Stewart. Can I get you anything to drink?" asked Jay.

"No sir, I am fine, but thank you."

"Stewart, we heard from Tiffany that you and Lisa were out a couple of nights before she disappeared and may have seen something suspicious. Tiffany indicated that Lisa had mentioned a car you didn't recognize?"

"Yes, sir, that was true. We had gone to the spot where kids like us go to make out. After we were, uhm, through and ready to go, a car turned around as though it was leaving but stopped and had its headlights on us for a little longer than necessary. We ducked down in case it was someone we didn't want to see us, but we were probably a second or two too late. It was eerie. I didn't recognize the car as belonging to anyone we hung with, but I didn't get a good enough look at it because of the lights to tell what make or model it was; I guess I'm not much help."

"Did you feel they were watching or scouting you out?"

"I don't know the answer because it's never happened before. It could've been perfectly innocent. It could've been someone who had gotten a new car, or their parents had; I'm not sure. Are we in trouble for it?"

"No, Tiffany told us this without her mother in the room, so your parents won't know unless you tell them if you are worried about that."

"Thank you, but I am worried about Lisa. I promise you that everyone I hang with, including my family, is concerned."

"I do have to ask you, since you are considered Lisa's boyfriend, where were you when she went missing, say between two and five?" asked Jay.

"Let's see, that would be Friday afternoon? I believe I was at home, probably playing video games."

"Anyone that can corroborate it?" asked Jay.

"Yes, my mother and sister."

"Okay, you are free to go. Here's my card. Call me if you think of anything else."

Stewart stood, pocketed the card, shook Jay's hand, and left the station. He was glad the interview was over. He felt like he was in a *Forensic Files* episode. But then his mind went to Lisa, and he wished he knew something helpful. His mother told him to pray for her. He decided to stop at the church on the corner and see if it was open. He felt an overwhelming urge to be on his knees in a serene setting.

He went to the Presbyterian Church nearby and found the chapel empty but inviting with the lights on low. He sat on the first pew and had his head in his hands for a long time, just evaluating his life and the things he had done that weren't pleasing to God. He was a jock, at least that was what his coaches called the football team, but he knew he was more than that.

He was responsible for getting a good education and doubted he would get a football scholarship. He knew his parents wanted him to go to college, but he also knew they struggled sometimes and may not be able to pay for it. He spent time with his grandfather in New Jersey last summer. His grandmother had passed away, and his mom wanted him to know his grandfather better. His grandfather had been a welder but was retired now. He still had his welding tools, and he showed him the basics. He enjoyed using his hands. He followed his grandfather's instructions and found using the tools was quite a skill.

He used to think that getting a degree in finance or something similar was the way to go. With the economy being what it was, he paid more attention to his future prospects and believed getting a practical education made more sense. He lifted prayers for Lisa and asked the Lord to help him with decisions about his future. After a little while, he left and went home. He still planned on going to the vigil tomorrow night. He only wished he knew if the car that shined its lights on them had anything to do with her abduction. His mind was going to dark places, which sometimes happened when he felt stressed. He knew the video games he still played weren't good for him. He made a conscious decision to look for a job and quit hanging out playing video games with his friends. He decided it was time to grow up. He wanted to make his parents proud.

chapter

28

Jeffrey was getting nervous about the abduction. He felt the FBI was looking at him hard. He thought he was being surveilled and wondered if his car could have a GPS tracker. He would check himself, but his mechanical skills were non-existent. He didn't want to take his car to his mechanic for apparent reasons. If a tracker were found, he may suspect him for several reasons. A Catch-22 situation. He decided to go to the airport instead and rent a car. He would tell Stella he had to put the Mercedes in the shop for service. He planned to leave it at the airport until he escaped this mess.

They missed the small window of opportunity to get their captee to the Norfolk port boat at the Norfolk, albeit that was a big lift. Now, they must try to transport her to Wilmington or maybe Charleston for the next transfer. He contacted the captain, who estimated they would be in Charleston in about ten days. He told him the weather was spotty, and he could do between 20-25 knots right now. "The closer I get to warmer weather, the wind should slow down, and I will pick up speed. Call me in a day, and I can give you a better prediction. Also, Wilmington isn't always available, so be prepared to go to Charleston as we get closer."

"I had hoped for Wilmington, but if it has to be Charleston, that's fine. It will take me at least a week to go by yacht. I'll call you tomorrow to see where you are and how the seas are faring."

Jeffrey would typically stay on the ICW. However, he didn't want to risk being seen, as there were more chances for the Coast Guard to detect them. Before going to the islands, he had gone out in the Atlantic, so he knew the nautical paths well.

He went by the safe house this morning to ensure everything was ready. They must leave by midnight tomorrow night to get to Charleston in time, assuming he can use his yacht.

When he arrived, he used the key code to enter and found Gil and his wife, Vera, in the kitchen having coffee. "Where is the girl?" Jeffrey asked after pouring his coffee.

Vera spoke up, "We have her in the back bedroom. She is tied to the bed with cuffs. They are more escape-proof."

Gil said, "She is a wild one, just like the previous guys said; she had to be medicated often to keep her from kicking the crap out of us. She had refused her food but finally ate a sandwich and drank the water. There's a toilet next to her bed. We can't trust her to cooperate by taking her to the bathroom."

"That's a good idea. The vessel won't be in port for a couple of days. I just spoke with the captain, and he was having rough seas right now but will give me a better estimate tomorrow. Hang in there and keep her blindfolded."

"We do," said Vera.

"Do you want to see her?" asked Vera.

"Yes, please," said Jeffrey.

Vera pulled up her laptop, which had the camera of Lisa's room. All Jeffrey could see was a girl lying asleep on a bed. Her left ankle was cuffed to the end of the bed, and her left arm was also attached to the bedframe. "I detach her from the ankle bracelet, and she pivots to the commode."

"Good plan; sorry she is so wild. We usually break them by this time. She will be in for the surprise of her young life. I can see she's a good-looking girl. My contact will be pleased," said Jeffrey.

Jeffrey called Britt Clayton on his burner phone when he returned to his car.

"Hi, what is going on?" Britt asked Jeffrey.

"It is getting close. I have been in contact with Cobbler. We missed the time slot in Norfolk, so now we are trying to get coordinated for Charleston. It looks like Wilmington is too unpredictable."

"How is the girl?"

"Wild, obnoxious, just started eating and drinking, finally," replied Jeffrey.

"Do you think Gil and his wife can handle the transfer? This is tricky. The pros are not this difficult. They are ready to go. I remember the last one Vinnie picked up. She was eager. Didn't Vinnie even say she asked him to have sex with her?"

"Yeah, he says he didn't, but sometimes I wonder. Are you going to be in town during this ordeal? I mean, I may need some support here," said Jeffrey.

"I plan to be. Call me on this number. I will keep it open. When is the transfer?"

"Probably tomorrow night or the following. It will depend on what the Captain tells me tomorrow. If I take my yacht, it will take me at least a week to get to Charleston if there is decent weather. I am hoping it works out. Depending on the ship's schedule, it could get pushed out."

"Got it, good luck." Britt hung up.

Katarina contacted Eliza the day before, after her time with Jeffrey; she told her something was going down because she could tell he was as nervous as a cat in a room full of rocking chairs.

She told her their lovemaking usually lasted an hour or more, but it was barely a half hour. "Of course, he would not say what was happening, but he mentioned something about a ship captain, and she heard it again when she listened to the recording she had placed on her shoe. I'm sorry, Eliza, but that was all he said that was remotely associated."

Eliza was checking on ports along the East Coast. Of course, it could be any boat of any size, but her best guess was that it would be one of those ships with several girls at once. They are called 'party ships,' the girls are clueless until they are transported to a seafaring freighter and end up in another country. Time was not on their side. Eliza knew she had a short window but was developing a plan. She called Jay and told him what Katarina told her.

"Where are you now?" Eliza asked him.

"I just pulled into the station. The vigil is tonight, and I think one or both of us should attend. You know how they love to show up and see their handiwork," said Jay.

"I'll be there shortly."

chapter

29

Stella Edwards had almost been suspicious of her husband since she married him. She knew he was unsatisfied with their sex life and suspected he had regular affairs. She knew that was what happened when you married a powerful and wealthy man. Her mother had suffered the same fate.

She could gauge the house's mood whenever her mother and father were at home at the same time, which was not often. Her father was of Greek heritage and a chip off the old block.

She knew her grandfather, Theodore Makris, was of the same mindset. He was very wealthy. As the child of an immigrant, he was poor growing up and was driven to do well in school, so hopefully, he would have the where-with-all to start his own business. He became an importer of materials used in the fashion district, an easy enough gig since he had contacts back in Greece. As his business grew, he got into the fashion design side of it, and with that, he met many designers, which led to meeting many beautiful models. Her grandmother learned to ignore and accept the infidelity.

That attitude was passed to her daughters, of whom she had three. She also had two sons who went into the business and followed in their father's footsteps in every way. One of them committed suicide after he got one of the models pregnant, and she threatened to go to his wife. It was a big family scandal.

She fell into the same dilemma. She married a wealthy man who was a prominent heir to a cosmetic company. Her father was an excellent provider, and he was involved in the family business and hoped to be head of it one day. He was a loving father to her and her sister. His Achilles Heel was his weakness, just like his father and grandfather. He couldn't resist other women. Her mother was never enough. Stella could see the disappointment on her face whenever her father came home late or left on an unexpected business trip.

Her mother had been told by her best friend that her father had made a pass at her. It came to nothing, of course, but it still hurt her mother to hear that. She could never understand why she was not enough for him. She read all of the Betty Friedan books and had breast augmentation. Nothing she did seemed to matter. So she gave up and let her body and her looks go. Stella hated that her mother was so hurt and felt she must suffer from depression. She encouraged her to see someone, but her mother said, "For what? To find out I'm married to a CAD?"

Stella quit asking. When she met Jeffrey seven years ago, she was attracted to his looks and sexuality. She was very beautiful but wanted a husband who loved her for who she was, not her beauty. He swept her off of her feet. She learned that Jeffrey went all in when he wanted something or someone. She received roses every day for a week, and he made dinner reservations every night and hoped she would go out with him.

She was overwhelmed. She graduated from Vassar and was familiar with powerful, wealthy men. He told her she was beautiful. Her natural beauty helped, but she worked at it by working out and caring for her skin. It didn't hurt that her father was the head of the cosmetic company where she preferred to get her products.

He eventually wore her down. He asked, and she agreed to go to the Bahamas, where he had a condominium. She knew she would be sleeping with him, and it would be a test drive to see if they were compatible. When they arrived in Freeport, Nassau, Jeffrey arranged for a limousine to drive them to the condominium.

She wanted a shower once they were in the room since they would go to dinner soon. While she was in the shower, Jeffrey stepped in and wrapped his arms around her, cupping her breasts. He lathered up his hands, proceeded to wash her back, and made his way down her legs and then between her legs. She opened up and let him enter her from behind. She cannot say she was displeased, but Jeffrey was more than pleased. He could not get enough of her. His sexual appetite was never sated. She hoped she could keep him pleased.

After they genuinely cleaned up, they prepared for dinner and enjoyed a beautiful night at a restaurant with a trio performing music from the fifties and sixties. It was so romantic. Jeffrey got down on one knee on the dance floor and presented her with a rock. It was at least two carats; judging from what her friend had received, she thought she had a good eye.

She said yes and was moved by his wanting to please her. They enjoyed each other's bodies for the rest of the week. She performed in more positions than she thought were possible. She felt he was satisfied each time. She was on birth control, but he used a condom anyway. He promised once they were married, he would not use them. He kept his promise.

They were married three months later in a large ceremony at the First Presbyterian Church in her hometown of Clifton, New Jersey. The honeymoon was a two-week Mediterranean cruise.

She loved history and enjoyed the beauty of the sites they saw. It was her major at Vassar. She spent time in Paris and Rome during college, so she recognized many places and could tell Jeffrey about them. Jeffrey seemed only to enjoy having sex. She became so raw in her private parts that she had to refuse him a couple of times. Her mom warned her of getting what used to be called 'honeymoon cystitis.' She thought she probably had developed it.

She noticed Jeffrey would go to the casino downstairs after dinner, and he would get in later and later. She would bathe and be in bed reading when he would get in. He went straight to the shower, then came to bed. He would give her a peck but not initiate romance. She was suspicious, and when he was snoring one night, she got up and smelled his shirt and another woman's perfume. She also found several condoms in his travel shaving kit. *So much for not using condoms*, she thought.

After learning this, she knew she had married her father and grandfather. She would perform sex when he wanted it, but it was never the same as before she discovered the betrayal.

Stella had reason not to trust her husband due to his infidelity. She got over that a long time ago. Fortunately, they had not become pregnant, so there were no children in the picture that would keep her from leaving him one day. She enjoyed her freedom and the ability to shop anytime. She knew Jeffrey thought her shopping so much was wasteful, but she shopped out of boredom. Recently, since the FBI Agents had stopped by, she had grown concerned over the news report about the missing young girl.

She knew Cynthia Curtis from the Oakleaf Country Club. She had admired her from afar because of her benevolence. She had seen her lately on news reports about a Bill she was trying to pass. She was always up to date on all the political and social issues. The Bill would give all NC police departments the ability to initiate a search if they suspect child trafficking. She believes such a law should have been on the books long ago. Finally, someone with a brain and a heart found a way to get the Bill to the floor, and now it was due to be signed by the governor.

She planned to contact Cynthia today to thank her for her work and offer her services. She was passionate about the border crisis and the young girls and boys who were being brought into this country by single men, and the current administration was letting it happen. She had read that thousands of children were unaccounted for, and no one seemed concerned. She wondered, *how much more sinister can this country get?*

"Cynthia?"

"Yes, this is she. Can I help you?"

"This is Stella Edwards from the Club. I was calling to tell you how proud I am of you and your success in getting the Bill passed to help find child traffickers. It is such an important issue. Please let me know if there is anything I can do to help you in the future."

"That is so kind of you, Stella. I am humbled. I will keep you apprised; if there is anything in the future, I will call on you. Are you and Jeffrey planning on being at the club for the 4th of July Bar-B-Que?"

"I'm not sure about the 4th of July. I will talk with Jeffrey and see what, if anything, he has planned. Thank you for reminding me."

"Great, hope to see you there." She hung up. *Wow,* thought Cynthia, *I didn't see that coming.*

Stella felt good after calling Cynthia. It put her in a mood to start doing more volunteer work and less shopping. It would take up her time. She was also going to start going to church. She and Jeffrey used to go to the Presbyterian Church close to their home, but when the pandemic hit, it closed, and they never returned. She planned to start going, regardless of whether Jeffrey wanted to go. It was too important to her, and the world needed more prayers than ever.

Jeffrey entered the front door and laid his attaché on the foyer table. He seemed to be in a hurry. Stella startled him when she came out from the kitchen. He looked at her like he had seen a ghost.

"What is it? You look scared," said Stella.

"You just startled me."

"Well, I do live here, too."

"I know, I didn't mean it like that. You are usually out at this time of the day. I didn't expect you to be at home."

"I decided to make some calls this morning rather than go out. By the way, had you planned anything for the 4th?"

"No, do you have anything in mind?"

"I was talking to Cynthia Curtis, and she told me there was a Bar-B-Q at the Club and wondered if we were going."

"Why were you talking with her?" asked Jeffrey, looking startled.

"I just called to congratulate her on the Bill she helped pass in the State House. She is quite the advocate. I admire her. Is there anything wrong with her?"

"No, no, of course not. I was just surprised you knew her," said Jeffrey, attempting to calm down.

Stella eyed him carefully. He seemed nervous. "Do you want to go to the Club? If so, I would need to call and make a reservation."

"I think it would be fun. Yes, sign up for it, please." He headed for his office and closed the door.

"By the way, darling, I had to put the Mercedes in the shop," he called back to her. "It had a knocking noise that I could not identify. I rented an SUV for a couple of days."

"I think we should go to the vigil tonight at the high school for the missing girl. Would you agree?" asked Stella.

"Sure, of course. What time is it?"

"Eight o'clock."

"That's fine, but would you please drive?"

"Yes, I would be glad to," said Stella.

They left at seven-thirty to drive to the high school. Stella drove the speed limit. She had gotten so many speeding tickets in the past that she was once about to have her license revoked. That scared her, and she started slowing down. She realized that it was a much nicer drive. *After all, what did she have to be in a hurry for? The nail salon? Huh!* she thought.

When they arrived, it was hard to find a parking spot. They had to walk quite a distance to hear the speakers. They heard Lisa's father thank everyone for the prayers and all the work put into finding his daughter. Her mother stood beside him but held onto his shoulder and leaned on her oldest daughter.

chapter

31

Trent and Michelle were about to do the hardest thing they had ever done: plead for the safe return of their youngest daughter, Lisa. They had spent the day with their pastor, Reverend John Marchant. John had provided support from the beginning, being there as a shoulder to cry on and to assure them with comforting words, sometimes bible verses, but most of the time, what was on his heart. They were grateful they had a supportive group of believers and friends around them during this stressful time.

They had been regular churchgoers all of their lives and did their best to steer their children in that way. Their prayer now was that Lisa had used her belief in God to get her through and that whatever was meant to be, they would all be able to handle it with God's help.

The vigil was to start at eight o'clock. A group of Lisa's friends, spearheaded by Tiffany and her friends, used social media to get the word out about the vigil. Trent knew they expected him to speak first, but he had not been able to prepare any words. He planned to speak from the heart.

As familiar faces gathered close to the makeshift stage, Trent took the microphone with Michelle, Brent, and Linda at his side and began to speak the words a father never wants to say.

"Thank you all for coming. The reason we are gathered here is a sad one for my family. First, we thank everyone who brought food, sent cards, and hugged us when we needed it most. Also, thanks to those who called at just the right time to give encouragement. We spent today with our pastor and have been on bended knee since this ordeal began. We were comforted by his words and knew everything that could be done was being done to find Lisa. We love her very much and want her to return home.

"I don't have anything more to say except to encourage all of you to continue to pray. If you think of anything that might help, please don't hesitate to speak up, no matter how trivial you think it might be. I can't thank Sheriff Taylor, the two FBI agents, and the deputies who have worked around the clock for a resolution. I am encouraged and confident that everything is being done. Time is not our friend, so the sooner we find her, the better."

Trent looked around, found Sheriff Taylor on the stage, and motioned for him to speak.

Sheriff Taylor gave an update on the investigation without giving out too much. He reiterated what Trent Williams said about speaking up if there is anything anyone knows that would help them. Then he stepped aside.

Tiffany Armano approached the mike, thanked everyone for coming, and started singing *Amazing Grace* while most everyone joined her. People had the candles that were passed out earlier and began lighting them. By the end of the song, everyone's candle was lit, and it was a sea of flickering lights against the backdrop of a high school where most of the kids attended. Tiffany thanked everyone again for coming and concluded the vigil.

Agents Mancini and Camp were in civilian clothes, observing people in the crowd. Both of them noticed Jeffrey and Stella Edwards toward the back. They both took notice but didn't mention it. It was a small town, and it would have been noticed if they had not attended.

Cynthia Curtis attended by herself to pay her respects. She didn't know the family well but realized they must be hurting. Stewart Mankiewicz was there with his parents and sister. He saw many other students hanging out and wondered what they were saying. He hoped they didn't suspect him.

It probably was well-known that he and Lisa were an item by the end of the school year. They were not very interested in each other except for the sex. That was the way Lisa was. She went from one guy to another. Now that he thinks about it, he was not comfortable with casual sex. It was just one of the things stupid kids did, and he did not feel stupid. He would change his ways and expected to get bullied about it in the new year. He would not want to wish it on anyone, but perhaps what happened to Lisa would be a wake-up call to the rest of the student body. Life was too short to do stupid things you would regret later.

When Stella and Jeffrey arrived home, Stella told him she just wanted a bath and then to go to bed. She felt melancholy after such a sad ceremony. "How did you feel about it?"

"It is so sad for the family. They have to be going crazy wondering where she could be."

"Do you think she got snatched to be sex trafficked?" asked Stella.

"No, I don't. I think some sicko decided to snatch her to be his little girl. You know, some people do that. Remember the case of the girl who got kidnapped and held for many years, even had a couple of children by her captor? I think it was in California."

"Yes, I do remember that case. You could be right. It sounds similar."

"Don't worry your pretty little head about it." He walked up to Stella, wrapped his arm around her waist, and kissed her deeply. Stella reciprocated as he felt her right breast. She knew he wanted sex tonight. It had been a while, and surprisingly, she was in the mood, too. While Stella was taking her nightly bubble bath, Jeffrey got a text from the ship captain that they had run into some rough weather and were delayed. He promised to update him again the next day.

After Stella had bathed, she put on her light blue negligee, which Jeffrey had given her for Christmas last year. He was looking at his phone in bed, but he set it aside when she crawled into her side. He rolled over to her side of the king-size bed and, without her objection, started removing the straps on her gown. She noted that he had changed his preferences. He used to be a leg and rear-end kind of man, but lately, he had started paying more attention to her breasts. She feels like it must be the influence of his other lovers, but now, she doesn't seem to mind. He was a tender lover for a change. He must have picked that up from one of his other lovers. She knew he had a number of women he called regularly.

She didn't mind much. She understood how men in power could be, so she accepted it as her lot in life. Tonight was as enjoyable a night as she had had in a very long time. Hopefully, he enjoyed it as well and will stop straying. If only.

chapter

32

"What the hell do you mean, she escaped?" screamed Jeffrey, trying to keep his voice down so Stella would not hear him. She was still in bed asleep. They had a very romantic night. He was still slightly mystified about why she would contact Cynthia Curtis, but first things first.

"She apparently had kept a nail file she asked for a couple of days before," said Gil. "Vera gave it to her and forgot about it. She managed to get the cuff off her wrist and fit her foot through the other cuff. It was amazing. She pretended to be in the cuffs when we went in to help her. We gave her privacy to go to the bathroom, so it wasn't noticed. She climbed up on the nightstand and got the window open. She was powerful and must have lifted herself up and out of the window. She had quite a drop and had to hurt her feet since she had no shoes. We are trying to find her, believe me."

"I believe you, but this is a disaster. If she can identify anything, then we are in serious trouble. I will call Vinnie and Walter and get them there to help look for her. The house is too far off the highway for her to make it anywhere to get help, so time is on our side, but we don't have a minute to waste. Keep your phone open."

E. L. Boyer

Next, Jeffrey called Vinnie. When he answered, he said, "Vinnie, you need to get to the safehouse now. Take Walter with you; no time to waste. Our little captee has escaped. It has been about an hour, so we have time to find her. Just hurry and keep me in the loop. I am on my way over there, too."

Jeffrey gathered himself and walked into the kitchen. He went upstairs, gently kissed Stella on the cheek, and told her he needed to go out for a little while but should be home soon. He said he would pick something up for breakfast so not to worry about him. "I'll bring you something home if you like."

"It's okay. I'm not very hungry. I will eat fruit. I may be in the bed when you get home. I had a tiresome day yesterday."

"Do you feel okay?" he asked her.

"Yes, I feel fine, just tired."

"Okay," he said and left the bedroom.

Jeffrey drove the speed limit but tried to push it to get out to the farmhouse property as quickly as possible. He was hoping she wouldn't have made it to the road. The house sits way back off a dirt road, at least a mile from a paved road. It was stark out there, though, so he hoped his phone was charged enough, and the same for Vinnie and Walter. He was so aggravated with Vera right now that he didn't want to speak to her for fear of losing his temper. She was his link to keeping the girl until they could transport her. He needed Vera more than he wanted to admit.

Once he drove down the gravel road, he could see the three cars and van in the driveway ahead. He jumped out and yelled for Vinnie and Walter. They came running up and said, "We found her! She had almost reached the paved road but walked slowly since she didn't have shoes. She fell once after tripping over some lumber. She scratched up her knee pretty bad."

"Thank goodness that was all. Knees will heal. Do you have a first aid kit?"

"Yes, sir. Vera is bandaging her up while Gil is holding her in place."

"Do you have flex cuffs?"

"Yes, sir, and we will use them on all her limbs. How much longer will it be before she is transported? She is getting wild. We are going to drug her again to get her back in bed. We all need a break after all of this excitement."

"Make sure she is monitored more closely. I am working on transport. If everything works out, we will move her in a few days. I am monitoring the ship's progress. After that, we can rest easy. She will be off of our hands. Are you two up for a trip while moving her? There is a bonus in it for you."

"That won't be a problem," said Walter while Vinnie nodded.

"I'll give you a call if we think we need you. Everything is up in the air, waiting on my contact to give us direction."

Jeffrey arrived home around ten o'clock. The house alarm had been set, so he had to disarm it. He was still driving the car rental. He hated to lie to Stella about the reason, but he was uncomfortable getting the Mercedes back. His nerves were shot, and even though it was still morning, he poured himself a scotch to calm his nerves. He never wants to deal with an underage girl again. He had not realized how high profile this one was when Vinnie said he had picked her out. He can't blame Vinnie. He wouldn't have known who Lisa Williams was, either.

He worried about having the two FBI agents nosing around. Walter and Vinnie were not very aware of their surroundings when making plans. Walter lived near the property where the plan was created, and they were overheard. They wouldn't have expected someone to overhear them because it is so lonely. This little project had been a hot mess all the way around. It seems he gets all the aggravation while Britt receives all the benefits. But he will get his reward. It was pretty lucrative; he had been told the younger they were, the higher the payoff. He was also finding out how high the risks were.

chapter
33

Agent Camp hadn't seen anything about Jeffrey's car on the GPS for a while. He looked it up and discovered why. It had been parked at the airport for the last two days. He knew now that Jeffrey was involved. Otherwise, why would he have left his car at the airport? He figured he rented a car for a while. He decided to see if he could catch him this morning, hopefully leaving in another vehicle. He went to the house and waited across the street in front of a neighbor's house, but no one ever came out. It was now lunchtime, so he figured they were already gone or were not leaving today. He had too many other things to work on, so he drove to the Sheriff's office. He needed to call Walter and make an appointment for him to come in and be interviewed. He called Eliza first and told her he was on his way to the meeting and that he discovered Edwards had left the Mercedes at the Raleigh airport parking.

The task force met at the hotel's command center to review everything and see what they were missing. Locating the truck had not panned out because everyone in Blaylock County owned a truck, well almost everyone. And on top of that, they were nearly all black or dark. Jay wondered if people were unaware that white was a safer color or if maybe they didn't care.

It was approaching one in the afternoon, and he just made it in time. Sheriff Taylor was there. He had been reinterviewing Lisa's friends, but it hadn't garnered more information. They were still in shock. Her boyfriend, Stewart, had called daily to see if there had been any news.

They went around the table and told where they were in the investigation. Rating on a one to ten scale, they were not even at half where they needed to be. This was their seventh day, including the day she was kidnapped. No ransom note was sent, so they ruled out that angle. The intense feeling was that she was taken to be trafficked.

Eliza told them trafficking was the most likely scenario. "I have several contacts up and down the East Coast and will notify them. Does anyone else know of another way?" No one seemed to have any other ideas.

Sheriff Taylor said, "We have interviewed all of her friends, and the ones she was with at the mall have been interviewed twice. We have interrogated her boyfriend. The key was Jeffrey Edwards."

Eliza said, "I agree, and Agent Camp and I are on him. We have a listening device in the home and were tracking his car, but we have since learned it is at the airport, so he is driving a rental. There has to be a plan to transport her to a boat or some vessel on the East Coast. The flesh peddlers have found they are at the least risk if transported that way. If they can get her on one of the vessels, then there is no telling where she can end up. Bimini is a hotbed for human trafficking."

"How do we avoid the transfer before she will be lost in the trans-Atlantic transfer?" asked Sheriff Taylor.

"Find her before she gets transferred. I will ask my contacts what the maritime records show for large vessels coming through. Hopefully, we have not missed our opportunity."

"Was there anything on the videotapes we could have missed," Kellum asked the deputies who reviewed the tapes.

"We went over all we had at least three times. That is, each of us did that. So, at least six eyes on each available tape three times," said Todd.

"Agent Camp, anything on the audio from the Williams' home?" asked Sheriff Taylor.

"No, sir. I have monitored during the day and every night. The only thing was his wife's conversation with him about the 4th of July party at the Club. She had learned from Cynthia Curtis, and Mr. Edwards seemed surprised that his wife would have called Cynthia Curtis. Then, his wife asked to go to the vigil, and he readily agreed. On another front, Mr. Edwards' handyman, Walter, is coming in this afternoon for an interview. Also, there were no usable prints on the gate lock at the Edwards property, where we think Angela overheard the abduction plan. I didn't think there would be, but it was worth a shot."

"Okay, no problem. Please let us know how that interview goes. And would you mind seeing Mrs. Curtis to see what she knows about the Edwards since Mrs. Edwards contacted her?"

"Great idea; will do," said Agent Camp.

chapter

34

After the meeting, Agent Camp called Mrs. Curtis to ask if she would allow him to come by or if she would instead come to the Sheriff's office. He got her voicemail, so he left a message. Since he had no other appointments, he decided to check with Eliza to see if she needed help checking the Maritime Records.

Eliza was on the telephone with her contact in Wilmington. Once the call ended, she smiled and told Jay she thought a pick-up point could be tomorrow. "Usually, they will be transported by a smaller vessel and then put on a cargo ship at Wilmington or another large port.

Then, they are transported again when they get to Charleston or Jacksonville. It depends on the type of craft they were using. The larger the craft, obviously, the harder it was for the port authority to check every corner. They use K9s, but the human transports were hidden so well that it was difficult for the K9s to sniff them out.

Homeland Security had quite a way to perfect their sensory efforts, but they were better than they used to be. It used to be so easy to transport, but at least now they have better tracking in their IT departments and have trolls watching internet traffic to catch these bastards."

Jay's phone rang. "Hello, Mrs. Curtis. Thank you for returning my call. Yes, three o'clock would be fine. I will see you then."

"Sounds like you have a date," said Eliza.

"Yes, I will try to find out what she knows about the Edwards'."

"I'll catch up with you later this afternoon, " said Eliza.

"I'll be back at the station by four-thirty. Remember, Walter is coming at five."

Jay arrived at the Curtis home on time. He was impressed with the immaculate grounds and said to Cynthia, "Your home is beautiful."

"Thank you. My late husband was a stickler for having a nice lawn. I have tried to keep it up. Of course, I am too old to do the mowing, so I have a gardener who comes once a week to do what is needed. I don't know what I would do without Jose. My late husband hired him when he was just a kid, but he grew up and started his own landscaping business, and now he has quite a large company. We were proud that he gained the confidence to make a living for himself and his family. My husband helped him by doing all of his legal work pro bono. He was a wonderful man, and I miss him every day. Come on in. May I get you something to drink?"

"Yes, I would appreciate a glass of water if it is not too much trouble."

"None at all. She went to her cupboard, got him a drinking glass, and filled it with ice and filtered water."

"Thank you very much."

"Now, how may I help you?" asked Cynthia.

"You know about the missing girl, Lisa Willams?"

"Yes, it is terrible."

"Well, this pertains to her; however, I would like to know how well you know Stella and Jeffrey Edwards."

"I know nothing about them. She called me out of the blue a couple of days ago to congratulate me on the Bill that passed. We chatted a little, and I reminded her of the 4th of July Bar-B-Q at the country club. We didn't talk for long. Is something wrong?"

"No, nothing is wrong. We are following up on leads as they come in, and his name came up as owning some property where one of our witnesses had overheard something."

"What did they overhear?" Cynthia asked curiously.

"That is privileged. I am sorry, but there are things we have to keep close to the vest. I'm sure you understand."

"Yes, I do. As mentioned earlier, my late husband was a lawyer, and my son was also a lawyer. I know some things must be kept private until the case ends. I sure hope they find that poor girl soon. I pray for her every night."

"I'm sure the family appreciates your concern. Here's my card. Please don't hesitate to call me if there's anything else you think of, okay?"

"Absolutely," said Cynthia.

Jay stood to leave, and Cynthia dropped a bombshell. "You do know that Jeffrey Edwards has property all over Blaylock County? I don't think most of it is rented or even lived in. I have often wondered why he had so much of it. He is a hedge fund manager; he must be waiting for the market to get hot again. I said I didn't know them well, but I had heard that much about him. You know how people talk, especially when it is about money."

Jay stared at her, but his wheels started turning. He almost stammered but recovered and said, "We knew he had some property. Now that you mention it, I will look into what he owns."

Cynthia walked him out on the porch and dropped another bombshell: "He also keeps a yacht in New Bern. It isn't huge, not like the one Trump had, but large enough. He named it after his wife, The Stella Queen. He added Queen, I think, just to be a little sarcastic. She had a 'Queen' air about her," she laughed. He didn't.

They said their goodbyes. Jay couldn't wait to get back to the station.

Agent Camp's heart was beating a million miles a minute as he got in his car and pulled his phone out to call Eliza. "You're not going to believe this!"

"Okay, try me," said Eliza.

"Jeffrey Edwards owns a yacht he keeps in New Bern. He also owns several properties all over Blaylock County."

"That's it. That has to be his connection. I was trying to figure out how he would transport her to meet in Wilmington. A party yacht or any other cargo ship would be too large to dock in New Bern. Jay, you're brilliant," said Eliza.

"Now we just need to locate where he is keeping her. I will contact New Bern Patrol to find out where he keeps a yacht. There are several Marinas there so that it might take a while. We could surround his yacht easily once we locate it. He's smart enough to have an alternate plan if he realizes his transportation is compromised, so we will need to be covert."

"I will put Todd on getting a listing of all of his properties. We will have to search them one by one. I hope it is not more than the department can handle. We will have to call in additional agents. I don't suppose he is back driving the Benz?"

"No, it is just sitting at the airport. I haven't caught him in another car yet," Jay told her.

"I'll be in shortly for the appointment with Walter."

"Okay, I'm going to update the Sheriff. He just walked in, and he looks pale. I need to go. Will catch you later."

"Sheriff Taylor, do you have a minute? Is there something wrong?" asked Eliza.

Kellum walked over to the makeshift desk she had commandeered. He sat down next to her. "Michelle Williams was just rushed to the hospital after her daughter found her unresponsive."

"Oh, no. Do they know what happened?" "Not yet. I called my wife and asked her to go to the hospital and stay with Trent. She knew Michelle from a Bible study class."

"I sincerely hope she will be all right," said Eliza. I have some news on the case, though, and it is good news. It is something we can work on and hopefully bring a conclusion to a terrible situation."

"What is it?" asked Kellum.

"Agent Camp found out through Cynthia Curtis that Jeffrey Edwards owns property all over Blaylock County. None of it was leased that she knew of; she thought he was only an investor. The best news was that he owns a yacht in New Bern."

"Wow, I had no idea he was that wealthy. How are we handling it? Sorry, but I had to go to Williams' home this morning, so I was out of pocket. Bring me up-to-date so I can help."

"After I locate his yacht, I will get agents to go to the marina in New Bern and get eyes on it. It may take time to find out if it is kept there. He could have registered it in a corporation or his wife's name. Some high rollers like to do that for IRS purposes. We have seen everything."

"Okay, good plan. What can I do now to help? I want to find Lisa, then deal with these cockroaches," said Kellum. His expression was with vitriol spilling out of his every word.

"If you could get Todd to look up every piece of property in the Edwards' names and then get officers to fan out looking for signs of her, it would be a huge help. This is going to be all hands on deck."

"Consider it done."

Kellum called Todd on his speaker. He was patrolling near the shopping center. "Yes, sir?"

"Todd, would you come on in and help with some lookups? We have a lead on a yacht in New Bern and other properties. You probably will have to get help looking all of it up, so let me know once you get here, and we will coordinate it. It is imperative we locate any hole in the wall in this county where Jeffrey Edwards has a property deed. It's looking more and more that he could be guilty of her kidnapping."

"I'll be there soon."

"Copy that."

chapter

35

Sheriff Taylor was in his office arranging his day planner. Eliza popped in with news about the information she received about the ships destined to stop in Wilmington and Charleston.

"The largest one is a party ship owned by a conglomerate out of Saudi Arabia."

"What makes it a 'party ship'? I am not familiar with that terminology," Kellum asked.

"We have had some success infiltrating the shipyards out of New York, and the Mafia have given some information about how these large ships show themselves. Tickets are purchased for a cruise down the East Coast with several stops. The men are promised a good time, if you get my drift. This activity is legal as long as all parties are of age and are not in a compromised position; however, it was well-known that many of the 'ladies' were being held against their will and were used for sex purposes only. They were told they must pay off their keep, but they never seem to do so."

"Do these women know fully what they are getting into when they sign up?"

"That is the question. We have been unable to get close enough to the 'ladies' to find out. It isn't easy. Ships beyond US boundaries have much less chance of being infiltrated by US Feds, Marshalls or FBI."

"I was just at a convention last year about human trafficking; however, I don't remember anything about this coming up," said Kellum.

"It is a very well-kept secret in the bureau. We have to hold cards close to the vest to help the passengers on board," Eliza told him.

"How did you get involved? What is your interest?"

"Jay told me you might ask me about it, and that is okay. I don't have a problem discussing it. My cousin was taken on a trip with her mother and a friend when she was only fourteen. It happened while they were sightseeing in New York City."

"Was she found? What happened?" Kellum asked.

"She was never found. The police at first thought she was a runaway, but her mother convinced them there was no way. They went to the Empire State Building, and Ellen became separated from her mother while getting on the elevators. Ellen never exited the elevator when her mother and friend reached the top. Her mother went crazy and started yelling at security, and they would not let her back on the elevator right away. Since then, they have changed their protocols, but at that time, they had allotted a certain amount of time for how long people could stay. The elevators would go back down and bring up the next group.

"It took my aunt and her friend to make a 911 call before they would listen to her. They used their walkie-talkies and locked down the building, but it was too late by then. She was gone. My aunt stayed in New York for two weeks, but when nothing turned up, and there were no leads, she returned to their home in Virginia."

"And your aunt, what happened to her?" asked Kellum.

"She and my uncle were never the same. Their son, Nathan, was younger than Ellen. As you can imagine, he was doted on, but he was a good boy and grew up to be a wonderful man. He has his own family now. My aunt and uncle still live in the same house, and my aunt contacted the NYC precinct over the years, but nothing ever turned up. The detective finally told my aunt a few years later that Ellen may have been taken for human trafficking, in other words, as a sex worker. There are pictures of children on the dark web, but when she was taken, there were very few resources to find her.

"They put out alerts across Europe, Inter- pol, and all, but that was the best they could do. Ellen would be too old now. She was two years younger than me, putting her at thirty-seven. If she was still alive, she was probably in a foreign country. It was so sad. The toll it takes on families is unfathomable."

"Thank you, Eliza. I had no idea, and I am so sorry. We all have crosses to bear, but your aunt and uncle had the biggest one. We must get Lisa back, or the Williams family will never be the same."

"Okay, let me go over the rest of the information I have," said Eliza.

For the next half hour, Eliza gave Sheriff Taylor the name and destination of several vehicles stopping in Wilmington and Charleston. She told him she thought the pick-up point was most likely in Charleston. "They also pick up other male passengers, and some may disembark."

"How can we monitor what was going on the ship?"

"That is another good question. We can't, so we must try to get to the vessel that will take her to the point of origin. We are trying to find out where Edwards has his yacht in New Bern. There are many marinas there. I have a contact covering the New Bern area since that is a hot transfer spot."

"I plan to go as soon as we locate his boat. If he doesn't use the boat, we are in a pickle; he could have an airplane connection we don't know about. Due to the distance, the most unlikely means of transport would be by car."

"Okay, what do you want me to do today?" asked Kellum.

"Could you spare one or two deputies to help search his properties? Todd has a list of at least a dozen. He can tell from Google Earth which ones have a dwelling so that we will search those first."

"Yes, of course. I've already told Todd to round some up to help."

"By the way, Jay called me last night and said Walter was a no-show. He has tried his cell several times, but he doesn't answer. He was working on getting a BOLO on him. He only wanted to talk with him. Walter must be involved up to his eyeballs. Have you heard how Mrs. Williams is doing?" asked Eliza.

"Holding her own. From what I understand, she had dehydration and a UTI, whatever that is."

"Urinary tract infection. My mother gets them all of the time. Probably from dehydration, too. She should pull through, but I'm glad they found her when they did," said Eliza.

chapter

36

J effrey told his assistant he would be out the rest of the day and to take messages but not have anyone call him. He knew he had a transfer to plan and had no time to work on his client's portfolios. He told Stella that morning he would be in meetings all day. He thinks his daily routine was covered, so he will unlikely be missed.

He called Cobbler on his SAT phone late last night to see when and where the transfer would occur. Cobbler was in constant contact with the ship's captain. He was unsure but is guessing another week. "If you are going to transport by sea, it is time to start. Put her in a shipping crate for transport; it is the least searched, and she will be safer.

He warned him that if they sensed feds nearby, he would raise the flag to half-staff; if he saw that, he would need to abort the mission. They would not take any chances.

Jeffrey told him he understood but wanted to know what he was to do with the 'product' if that happened.

"That's up to you," was all Cobbler would say. Jeffrey was feeling an enormous amount of pressure. With the prostitutes, he never had this issue. They were willing to take a cruise.

He was on his way to the safe house now. His other problem was

Walter. He hadn't shown up at the station the previous night and was now nervous he would be picked up. "I told you to go ahead and go to the interview, but just deny everything," Jeffrey told him.

"I know you did, but I got nervous. Do you think I should go in this morning and say I was too ill with the stomach flu?"

"Yes, go in this morning. Hopefully, the agent will take pity on you. Let me know what happens."

"I will."

When Jeffrey got to the safe house, Vera was in the room with Lisa. He talked with Gil about what he needed for the transfer. Gil told him he would go to the local hardware store and get what he thought would work.

"Just remember, whatever we put her in has to be porous so she can breathe."

"Yes, I know. We also have some blankets here that we could wrap her in to keep her warm."

Vera came up the stairs and heard the conversation. "I am not sending my grandmother's handmade quilt with that little bitch. She can freeze to death."

"No problem," said Jeffrey.

Jeffrey drove to his marina, which was an hour away. He wanted to ensure no other boats were leaving this afternoon. Going down the ICW would take about three hours, so they must get underway soon.

After he checked on his yacht and ensured he had a full gas tank, he went below and readied the last berth, where he and Stella stay whenever they use it. She wasn't fond of seafaring, so he had not been on any cruises lately, with or without her. He considered putting it up for sale after this venture. Vera and Gil have agreed to accompany him and keep the girl sedated for the transfer. He would rent them a car to return after they completed the mission. He planned to return on the yacht alone. He needed to call Stella and make an excuse for his absence; he wasn't sure yet what he would tell her.

His cell phone rang, and he saw it was Agent Camp. He declined the call and turned off his regular phone. He would use his burner for the rest of the day. Walter can wait until tomorrow.

He drove back to the safe house in time to see Gil unload a crate normally used to store fruit. On the back of the truck, he had a bale of hay and two very sturdy painter's cloths.

"What do you think, Mr. Edwards?"

"It looks like it will work. She is tall, but she can bend her legs and be comfortable. How much do I owe you?"

"I spent sixty-one dollars on everything."

Jeffrey handed Gil a hundred-dollar bill and told him the rest was for his gas and trouble. "You and Vera will be paid handsomely once the mission is completed. Would you check with her to see if the girl is ready? We need to get moving so we can get there on time."

"I'll be right back," said Gil.

chapter

37

Michelle Williams was being discharged from the hospital today. She was nervous about going home. The stress hadn't gone away. Lisa wasn't home, so she would face the world again without her youngest child. Her heart was full of sorrow but also hate. She knew she was going to have a breakdown if she didn't get some help. A hospital chaplain came to see her last night, and she was wonderful.

Her name was Judy Morrison, but she told Michelle to call her Pastor Judy. She had a warmth that made you want to melt in her arms. She read some verses from the Bible, in particular from Proverbs. Michelle wrote them down and told her she would reread them when she went home. She hoped that sometime in the future, she would be able to forgive her daughter's abductors, but right now wasn't the time.

She told Pastor Judy how she felt and assured Michelle that she understood and that anyone else would feel the same. However, she thought the spirit would move her to find joy and eventually make sense of what happened. "I know you want me to tell you everything will be all right, but I won't do that. Sometimes, things don't work out as we hope, and we have to be able to accept those things we cannot change."

She held Michelle's hand and said, "You and your family will be in my prayers." Then she left.

She didn't tell Pastor Judy how she spent at least an hour in Lisa's room daily, holding onto her favorite doll. It was the last doll she had received from her and Trent. She believed she was about eight years old that Christmas. She loved the doll and named it Hannah after one of the characters in the Harry Potter books she read as a child; a few months later, she told her mother she thought she had outgrown dolls. Her birthday was coming up, and she wanted to spare her mother from buying her another one. Michelle was heartbroken, but she understood. Her little girl was growing up. She kept it on her bed. It had blond hair and blue eyes like Lisa, and she wore a cute blue flowery dress, black patent shoes, and a white headband with a blue flower. Lisa kept her pristine. Once, Michelle wanted to update Lisa's room because she was entering her teens. She agreed to let her paint the room and change the comforter and curtains, but the doll had to stay. Michelle held the doll every day and cried. She so wanted Lisa back in her arms.

The nurse removed her IV so she could shower and dress. Her husband and daughter will be taking her home in about an hour.

Agent Camp was at the station when Walter walked in. He apologized for the night before. "I was not feeling well and had lost your phone number. I'm sorry."

"I'm glad you are here now, Walter. I was in the process of putting out a BOLO on you, and if that hadn't worked, I would have resorted to a warrant," Jay told him. "Let's go into the interrogation room."

Walter followed him and sat down in the chair facing the mirror. He had been in enough interrogation rooms to know they were watching and probably recording him.

Jay turned on the tape recorder and said, "Today is Thursday, June 29th, 2023, and this is FBI Agent Jay Camp interviewing," Jay motioned to Walter to state his name, which he did, saying, "Walter Green." Jay had Walter's driver's license in front of him.

"How long have you known Jeffrey Edwards?"

"Six years, give or take a little," said Walter.

"Are you employed by him?"

"Yes, I'm his handyman," said Walter. "And what all does that entail? What do you do for him if you can be more precise?"

"I do repairs at his home if they are simple, basic things. I can do basic electricity; nothing complicated. I'm not licensed. I don't do any plumbing. I can diagnose the problem, but then I'll call a plumber. I help him with his properties if they have a house or barn on them."

"How many properties does he have?" asked Jay.

"I believe there are six or seven that I know of."

"So he could have more?" Jay asked.

"Yes, sir. I don't need to take care of anything if there isn't a dwelling. So if there were just land, I wouldn't know about it."

"Fair enough. Have you ever known Mr. Edwards to use his property for nefarious reasons?"

"What does that mean?" asked Walter.

"Any reason that may be unlawful, something that didn't seem right."

"No, no, nothing like that," reassured Walter.

"Does anyone else have access to his properties?"

"I wouldn't know that." Walter was getting nervous, and when he did that, he tended to stutter, so he was trying to hold that back. He had watched enough ID shows with his wife and knew the law would trip you up if they thought they could.

"Have you been arrested before?"

"You know I have. It was a very long time ago when I was a teenager. Drunk and disorderly, they called it. It was a misdemeanor. Then, once a few years later, I was accused of shoplifting, but the charges were dropped."

"Why were they dropped?" asked Jay.

"The owner was my wife's employer, so he felt sorry for her and told the police he was mistaken and that I had paid for the merchandise in advance, and he didn't know it. I got lucky."

"So you admit you did shoplift?"

"I did. It was a perfume bottle for my wife, and I didn't have the money to pay for it. I was arrested and taken to the station. Then the owner came down, and they released me."

Jay knew he was telling the truth and could see he wouldn't get any more out of him. He was being very cautious. He told Walter he was free to go, and he handed him his card. "Call me if you think of anything."

When Walter stood to leave, Jay said, "One more question: where does Mr. Edwards keep his yacht, 'Stella'?"

Walter was caught off guard and said, "In New Bern, and it isn't Stella, it is Sophie, named after the dog his wife had when they married, but she died a few years ago."

"Thank you, Walter. You have been very helpful. Keep my card handy; I may call you again to come in."

Walter walked out the door, and Jay pulled out his phone and called Eliza. When she answered, he said one word, "Sophie."

"Yes, and?" asked Eliza.

"The name of his yacht, not Queen Stella but Sophie, after his wife's deceased dog."

"You are kidding. Right?"

"Nope, we need to get going," said Jay.

Eliza searched the maritime records she was perusing: Sophie, New Bern, NC, Jeffrey Edwards. Bingo. A picture of it came up. She ran out of her office, and Jay met her in the front lobby.

Sheriff Taylor heard all of the commotion and walked out of his office.

They both had smiles on their faces, and he knew. "Get going, I'll hold down the fort here. Call me on your way and give me the low down."

"Will do," reassured Eliza.

Jay said, "I'll drive." In another five seconds, they were on the highway headed to New Bern. He left the siren off for now.

"It's actually Sophie Marie," Eliza told him.

"Nice," said Jay.

chapter

38

Brent and Angela were at his house to welcome his mother home from the hospital. His dad and Linda had gone to pick her up. Angela had her mother make another lasagna, and she made a salad for them at their house.

Trent pulled up the driveway, and with his daughter's help, they walked Michelle up the front steps. Angela heard Michelle say, "I don't need any help," as she entered the front door. "I can walk alone. Y'all are making too much of a fuss."

They sat her on the sofa in the family room, and Trent went to the kitchen and got her a bottle of water. "Michelle, you know you need to drink more water, so please drink all of this," he handed her the bottle after he opened it.

Angela watched as Michelle took the bottle and nodded her head. She looked so broken. She felt sorry for her and couldn't imagine what her mother would do if she or her brother were missing.

Angela told them a lasagna dish was baking in the oven, and a salad was made and ready for them. She and Brent had decided earlier to go out somewhere tonight. They needed to be alone. She knew Brent was upset and wanted to be alone with him. They left shortly after, and Brent told his dad he would be home by midnight.

They went to a pizza joint in town and enjoyed their short time together. Some of Brent's friends came in and talked with them for a while. They assured Brent that Lisa would be okay. A boy named Stuart told him, "She's a fighter." Angela knew they were trying to comfort him, but she also knew they were as doubtful as all of them were. Time was dragging, and there didn't appear to be much progress.

Brent later told Angela he was sure Stuart and Lisa had been together romantically. "I knew Lisa was sleeping around. I heard the rumors but didn't confront her, which I should have."

"What good would it have done? You knew she had a mind of her own. You're not that kind of person, Brent. You are kind and loving. That's why I am with you," said Angela.

He kissed her, and they started necking. He reached into her top and felt her left breast, but that was as far as they went. As much as they lusted for each other, they knew they wanted to wait until they married. Angela hoped he wouldn't find anyone else when he went to college. She knew her prospects of college were almost nil. She would go if she could get a scholarship; otherwise, it would be too expensive, and she didn't want to borrow money. She had heard the nightmare stories of kids who took out student loans and couldn't repay them, or if they could, they had almost nothing left to live on.

After getting home, she showered and went to the kitchen for a glass of milk. She saw where Andy had left the back door cracked. His mother must not have noticed it. She closed and locked it. She will let her mother know in the morning. She then went to Andy's room and saw his head on the pillow, and he was facing the wall. She turned on his night light and closed his door. She then went to her mother's room and heard some sounds. She didn't want to scare her mother but wondered if she was okay. She waited a few minutes and heard her mother say, "I'm going to the bathroom and will be right back."

Angela rushed into her room and closed the door most of the way, leaving it cracked just a little. She saw her mother come out and go into the bathroom. Then, because her mother had left her door open, she noticed a man sitting on the side of the bed, and Angela had a full view of the bedroom.

She recognized the man as being their neighbor. He had just moved in about two weeks ago. She had only seen him outside on his porch at a distance. She guessed he was single or divorced. She hadn't noticed any children or signs of children like toys. She hoped he was a good one and not one of the losers she had in the past. Her reqret was that she had a male visitor overnight with Andy in the house. She could understand it, but Andy wouldn't. He was getting old enough now to ask questions. It just now dawned on her that was why the door was cracked. He walked over and came in the back so Andy wouldn't see him. He probably just got here.

She guessed her mother expected her home later than eleven. She and Brent were tired, so they called it a night at ten o'clock. Angela decided to go to bed. She knew her mother would have him out of there before they got up in the morning. Everyone had their secrets.

The following day, when Angela got up, her mother was already in the kitchen making Andy pancakes. She didn't have to work until eleven, so she had time to make breakfast.

"Hello sunshine, how are you?" her mother asked.

"I'm fine. Mrs. Williams looked good. I'm sure they enjoyed the lasagna. Brent and I went to get pizza and hung out for a while."

"I'm so glad she's back home. The problem is still there, though; her daughter is missing. I'm sure it was hard on her to walk into an empty house," said Brenda.

"I know. It was terrible. The police were due to give them an update sometime today. I believe this was the seventh day, maybe eighth, but who's counting?"

"They are," said Brenda.

"I hope they have some good news."

"So do I," called out Andy. He was sitting in front of the TV watching cartoons.

"Okay, little one, get your hands washed. It is time for breakfast. I have plenty, Angela. Do you want some?"

"Yes, please!"

chapter

39

Walter Green was having serious guilt over what he had done. He doesn't think the FBI was suspicious of him being involved in the actual abduction, but he knew it was just a matter of time.

Agent Camp was no dummy. He just needed to look at that video from the mall again, and he might then realize the person walking out with Lisa matched his stature. They must have already suspected it was a man who would have the strength to take over and change her appearance.

His wife, Sandy, was the sweetest woman in the world, and she doesn't deserve what will come down once they figure it out. They will get a warrant and destroy his home, looking for evidence. His nerves were frayed. He wasn't lying when he told Agent Camp he was ill the day before.

His relationship with Jeffrey Edwards came about only because he knew Vinnie. Vinnie was his wife's cousin's boyfriend. They met at, of all places, a family reunion about eight years ago. The cousin dropped him as a boyfriend, and she married another man. She did the right thing. Her husband was a hardworking logger, and they had twin boys they were crazy about. Sandy had babysat them a couple of times. He and Sandy haven't been able to have children. She was a hard worker, holding down two jobs to his half job. He knew he didn't bring much money into the relationship, but he was loving and kind to her and did other things to make it up to her. She never had to worry about getting a handyperson. He had been able to fix almost anything in their double-wide. Other people in their trailer park use his services, too. He didn't charge them much because he knew they were on fixed incomes. Most of them were elderly.

Both of his parents had passed away. Sandy's mother lived about five miles away. She had her own tiny home, which, fortunately, she had paid off. Sandy's father's life insurance, plus he was killed on the job. It happened when he stopped to help a motorist change a tire. He was a highway patrolman, and a wayward car hit him. She ended up with quite a large sum from life insurance plus a settlement from the insurance company of the person who hit him. She invested it well, and since she continued to get his pension, they were okay day to day. Sandy and her brother were both in high school, so she still had a lot of expenses to cover. She had assured Sandy and her brother that they would get a sizable inheritance one day.

Walter wondered if he turned himself in now; perhaps he would get a lighter sentence. He knew the girl was still alive, and the plans were underway to transport her, but he wasn't sure how. Since the agent tricked him into telling him about Jeffrey's yacht, now he thought perhaps they thought he was planning on transferring her by boat. If only he could be sure. He doesn't want to make a mistake and turn himself in prematurely if they don't suspect him. He had trouble making decisions. It had troubled and followed him all of his life. He was a poor student and had never had a real job. He was glad he watched and learned from his father about doing minor repairs. He had gone to a community college and learned basic electrical wiring and simple plumbing. His training was limited to just that.

His mother and father were good people. He was their only child. His father was a Vietnam Veteran and got cancer when he was in his fifties. It was Agent Orange-related. He died from liver cancer when he was only fifty-four. His mother was brokenhearted. She developed emphysema from smoking and died when she was only fifty- nine. He and Sandy were already married, and she was a great support. He loved his parents and missed them. They gave him anything he wanted. He had no siblings and wished he could have made them prouder of him.

Now, their only son was a child kidnapper and will probably go to prison for it. He had heard what they do to child killers in prison and thought it probably extended to kidnapping. It scared him to wonder if he would suffer the same fate. He believed he had decided what to do, no matter how much it hurt him and others.

❖ ❖ ❖

Jeffrey was back home, but just for a short time. He called Britt on his way and told him the transfer was to take place that night. He said they were bringing her to New Bern, but he was now concerned about using his yacht. He felt sure the FBI had been tracking his moves.

"I would like to use your brother's boat. It would ensure we wouldn't be caught. Would you call him and remind him he owes me a favor."

"I don't know, Jeffrey. He was very particular about who uses it. His boat captain is not available now because his wife had surgery for cancer. He would have to take it out himself."

"I don't care who drives it, Britt. Need I remind you that you are in on this venture and are as deep in it as I am?"

"Yes, I know."

"You know I did Christian a big favor when his company was about to go under. I invested heavily in it so that he could keep it afloat. I hate to pull the trump card now, but I have no other option."

"I'll call him now," said Britt.

In the meantime, Jeffrey called Gil.'

"Hello, there may be a change of plans. I can almost feel the FBI breathing down my neck. We may be going to a different marina tonight. It won't be any farther for you. I will send the information soon. Is everything still okay for the transfer?"

"So far. Vera has been her only contact so far. When she sees us coming to get her, she will probably start freaking out. We still have some sedatives to use on her."

"Okay, just be careful with the dosage. I don't want her to stop breathing."

"I will. Don't worry about that," Gil reassured Jeffrey.

He was getting a call on his burner and knew it was Britt. "Gotta go; will call you soon," said Jeffrey. He answered the burner. "Christian told me he will meet you, and y'all can drive together. Okay?" asked Britt.

"That will work. Tell him to meet me at the club at seven tonight."

"Listen, Jeffrey. Christian doesn't realize how deep I am into this business, so if you can minimize my involvement, I would appreciate it."

"Too late for that, sorry." He hung up. Jeffrey was thinking that Britt must be getting soft. This will be the end of their relationship, for sure.

Jeffrey called Gil back and told him to look for the coordinates, but it would come from another phone number, not his regular number. He was paranoid that they were listening in.

Jeffrey texted Gil the marina name, Montego Bay, and the address. He sent him the dock and slip number. "Pull up as close as you can, and we will carry her on using one of the luggage racks."

"Got it, boss."

chapter

40

Jay and Eliza arrived in New Bern with some daylight left. They went to the dock, where a yacht named Sophie Marie was docked, slip number twenty-one. There were no other yachts out, and they thought it was strange that there weren't many boats on such a beautiful day. They could see a few empty slips farther down from where they were. They visited the harbor captain's office and introduced themselves.

"Glad to have you here," said Captain Ellis.

"Why's that?" asked Jay. Eliza cocked her head waiting for an answer. She was petting the black lab, standing next to the captain.

"Well, I have been watching some activity going on around here recently, and with all of the drug problems we are having up and down the coast, I wondered if it was being transported out of New Bern. We are a bit out of the way and have mostly recreational boating, but there has been an alert from the U.S. Coast Guard to be on the lookout for suspicious cargo."

He looked around at his desk, found the notice, and posted it on the bulletin board. "I should have already done this; I just have been a little negligent lately; my wife is ill, and I have been busy taking her to appointments."

Eliza said, "I am sorry about your wife and hope she will be well soon. That notice is important, but we are concerned about another type of cargo. Human."

"Human?" Captain Ellis asked. "I haven't seen any activity to indicate that was going on here."

"What is your responsibility regarding the marina?" asked Jay.

"I am responsible for this one and the one next to us. There are over one hundred fifty slips. They are not all full right now, obviously. It is a fluid situation. Some are going, and some are coming. There is always something to be checking on and fixing."

"Anything ever going on with Mr. Edwards' yacht?"

"Let's see, that would be The Sophie Marie?"

"Yes, that's correct," responded Eliza. "I did see Mr. Edwards down there just yesterday. I felt he was checking it to ensure it would be ready to take out. They don't do much on it but cruise around for a day or two. Not very often, though. I don't think his wife is keen about being on the water."

"Does he take anyone else?" asked Jay.

"Occasionally, he has a couple of clients he will take, and he has let a client use it without him onboard, which is a little risky, but these people with money can afford it. You knew he was a hedge fund guy?"

"Yes, we were told. Okay, so he didn't sign in about taking it out?"

"No, but he doesn't have to do that. He pays for the slip year-round. He has it taken out to be cleaned in the winter season, but it's normally in the slip, ready to use at any time."

"Thank you, sir. We hope your wife is well soon and you have a good day." Jay gave him his card and told him to call if he noticed anything suspicious.

"What is your lab's name?" asked Eliza.

"Carly, she is a great dog, the best one we have had," he told her as he petted Carly's head. Eliza noticed that she was lapping up the compliment.

"What do we do now?" Eliza asked Jay.

"How about we go get some seafood?"

While they were waiting on their food, they went over a plan. Since it was almost dark and the ride back was two hours away, they decided to get a couple of rooms and wait overnight, then come back in the morning and see if the yacht was still in the slip. They had nothing else they could do tonight. They were working on the case around the clock and were out of ideas. Eliza said she would call her contact to get an update on the ports and what was expected. The weather was good, so she didn't think anything would have changed, but she wanted to double-check. "I'll update you after I talk with my source."

"Sounds like a plan. I need a good night's sleep, so don't call too late, or I might be snoozing," Jay laughed.

They walked around the town to get the lay of the land. Jay suggested The Captain's House motel. They were on a government employee's budget.

When Jay got in his room, he called Sheriff Taylor and updated him. "I don't think he is moving anything tonight. We will check again in the morning, and if all is cool, we will drive back tomorrow. Anything on surveillance?"

"I have nothing to report. His phone has been silent. He is probably using a burner to do most of his business."

"Copy that. See you sometime tomorrow."

Eliza called her source, who told her the Wilmington cargo ship would arrive tomorrow afternoon. "The other possibility is Charleston, and it is a cruise ship. A company in Qutar owns it, Arabic. It could be a party ship," she told her.

"Okay, so nothing new. I will check back tomorrow. I think we are on the right track. They must be shipping out of New Bern to Wilmington."

Eliza called Jay and updated him.

chapter

41

Jeffrey sat at the club's bar, looking at his watch. It was six-fifty-eight, and there was no sign of Christian yet. He hoped he would be there soon. They need to get on the road to meet Gil. Jeffrey was focused on a baseball game on the bar's TV until he felt a tap on his left shoulder and turned around. It was Veronica, one of his many girlfriends from college and one he was still seeing occasionally. It had been a while, and he was surprised to see her.

"How have you been?" Jeffrey asked her.

"Well, since I last saw you, I got married."

"Really? Wow, I didn't see that coming."

"I know. I thought I would stay single for the rest of my life, but he swept me off my feet. It was true love," said Veronica.

"I am very happy for you, but I will miss you, and I think you know what I mean."

"I do, and I don't blame you," she laughed. "Oh, here's Raymond now."

A tall, very fit man with dark hair graying at the temples walked over to greet them. "Raymond, this is my friend from college, Jeffrey Edwards."

Raymond reached out his hand and said to Jeffrey, "Your name sounds familiar to me."

"Well, I handle money if that helps jog your memory," said Jeffrey.

"Yes, it does. I have a couple of friends that have mentioned you. Maybe we could get together sometime?"

"That would be great. It's nice to meet you, and it's good to see you again, Veronica," said Jeffrey, handing Raymond his card.

Jeffrey looked at his watch as they walked away, ten after seven. He called Christian's cell number and got his voicemail. Jeffrey left a curt message that he needed to hear from or see him immediately. He then called Britt, and when he answered, he asked if he had heard from Christian.

"No, I haven't. He should be there by now. I hope nothing happened. I'll call him at his home number and see if he's there. I'll call you right back."

Jeffrey was seething by this time. He called Gil, and when Gil answered, he asked if he had left yet. "No, but she is loaded, and we are about to pull out. Is something wrong?"

"I don't know yet. Hang tight for a few minutes."

"Okay," said Gil.

He hung up and looked at Vera, and shrugged his shoulders. He and Vera had struggled to get the crate in the truck. Vera gave Lisa a shot of Valium, followed by Phenergan, to get her passed out enough so they could put her in the crate. It was a heavy dose, but Vera knew it wasn't sufficient to harm her. She had been an RN back in the day and gave these drugs regularly. She had worked on every floor of Baptist Hospital since graduating from nursing school.

She gave it up after she married Gil. She had already raised her two children, went through a divorce, and had been on her own for ten years. She was happy to get off of shift work. When she and Gil got together, he told her he worked for a wealthy man who lived in Raleigh but had business in Blaylock County, so he preferred to live in Blaylock

County. They moved into Gil's mother's house. Vera took care of her for two years until she passed. She missed his mom. She was a sweet lady and taught Vera how to cook and bake. She wished she had known her many years ago while raising a family. Her kids lived on fast food, unfortunately.

Gil's phone rang, and it was Jeffrey. All he said was yes sir and yes sir and hung up.

"Well, what did he say?" Vera asked.

"We're screwed," said Gil.

"What does that mean?"

"The yacht we were using is now out of play because the owner had an accident while driving to meet Jeffrey. They weren't sure he would make it, and Jeffrey wasn't sure what to do now. He feared using his yacht because he thought the FBI was watching it and we would be caught."

"You're kidding? I didn't work all of my life to go to federal prison for kidnapping. You told me this was foolproof, and we would make a lot of money."

"I know, I know, and I really thought it was. I am sorry. We are going to come up with another plan. Trust me, please," said Gil.

"What choice do I have?"

Vera got out of the truck and went to the back to see if she heard any noise from their captee, but it was all quiet. She reached in and felt her forehead, and it was warm. Then she went further in, touched her temporal area, and felt her pulse. She didn't think there was any problem with her. If there were much more of a delay, they would have to pull over on the way so she could be medicated again. She had hoped this wouldn't happen. She had been uneasy about giving her so much medication.

She returned to the truck and told Gil that the girl was okay. He told her he was still awaiting a call back from Jeffrey. His phone lit up just that minute, and he hit the green button. It was Jeffrey. "We are going to drive to Wilmington. It's the only way. The ship will pull in by four tomorrow afternoon; we will wait overnight. We may have to play it by ear. I'm on my way to your place now. I'll follow you to Wilmington."

"Okay, boss. We are sitting here waiting. The girl is asleep, and Vera is monitoring her. See you soon."

chapter

42

Walter had been having trouble sleeping. He worried that he and Vinnie would get caught if the Feds were already onto Jeffrey Edwards. He knew that Jeffrey had two FBI agents visit him. He had overheard Vinnie talking with him on the phone. Vinnie didn't seem worried. He had an out: He could lay low with his brother in New York. Walter had no other place to go. He was having a severe case of regret.

That morning, Sandy asked him if he was ill. He replied, "No, why do you ask?"

"You tossed and turned all night and have been doing that for several nights. Is there anything you need to tell me?"

"Oh, Sandy, I have messed up so bad. I was one of the kidnappers of Lisa Williams."

"You what?" she screamed at him. She started pacing the kitchen. She picked up her cell phone and began to call 911, but Walter grabbed her arm and told her he did not want her involved.

"I will go to the police station and tell them what I know, which isn't much. We took her and kept her for one night and a day until she was picked up by another party that I didn't know. They took her to another place, so I don't know where she is now."

"Then what good would it do for you to go to them?" asked Sandy.

"If I don't, she won't have a chance of being found. If I can at least give them my part, they can start trying to find her. I'm so sorry, Sandy. I know I am a big disappointment. Hopefully, they will go easier on me if I confess now."

"We will take out a second mortgage on the house and get you an attorney," said Sandy.

"Are you sure?"

"I love you, Walter. I am your wife, and we are going to stick together. I am going to check the directory and find a defense attorney. Just sit tight while I find the telephone directory."

Sandy came back, and they went through the directory and came across Martin Curtis and Associates. She called and got a very nice lady on the phone, and she explained the issue but didn't give too many details. She only told her that they needed a defense attorney to help them navigate the system when her husband confessed to a crime. The lady told her they had an attorney in the practice who could help with that, and they made an appointment for that afternoon at three o'clock.

At three o'clock, Walter and Sandy sat in James Sisk's office. Sisk began the conversation.

"Explain the circumstances and the nature of your need for a defense attorney, Mr. Green."

Walter looked at Sandy and then started telling James Sisk his woes. "I have committed a serious crime, and I know I will be arrested when I go to the sheriff's office, so I came to you first. My wife," he glanced at Sandy but continued, "found your firm and made the appointment. I'm glad she did."

James noted Walter's wife reached over and squeezed Walter's hand.

"Please tell me what you have done that you believe you will be arrested for."

"I helped in kidnapping Lisa Williams," said Walter in a matter-of-fact voice.

"Okay, we must immediately turn this over to the sheriff's department. Don't worry. You are entitled to a defense. I assume you are hoping for some leniency by turning yourself in now. Are you in possession of information that will help them find her?" asked James.

"Yes, sir. I believe I am."

Walter told James about the plot for the next hour and how he helped find a girl to kidnap. As noted by his attorney, his wife cut her eyes at him a couple of times. He explained how he did it and that he had a co-conspirator for the crime. He told him they kept her a little over twenty-four hours until another couple of men came to get her.

James asked him who was behind it and if he had received any payment.

"Jeffrey Edwards called on my partner to set it up, and my partner called on me. I have been Mr. Edward's handyman for his properties for a few years. I have not received my payment yet. It was to come after she was transferred to another party. It was human smuggling for sex, plain and simple."

James looked at Sandy and asked, "Mrs. Green, were you in any way involved, knowingly or otherwise?"

At that, Walter jumped up and loudly told James, "She had nothing to do with this. She learned I was involved when I confided to her this morning."

"What caused you to confess?" asked James.

"I had not been sleeping well, and she asked if I was ill. That was when I broke down and told her. She's my rock. I don't know what I would do without her. I messed up."

James looked at Sandy, and she nodded in affirmation. James Sisk picked up the telephone and asked his assistant to call the sheriff.

chapter

43

Brent and Angela were driving back from the mall to his house. They had gone to the mall to get his mother a new robe and slippers. Her birthday was tomorrow, and even though this was the worst birthday she had ever experienced, they would try and help her enjoy it. She still cries most of the day and spends time in Lisa's room every day. Trent, his father, had taken a leave from his workplace. He kept in touch with his brother every day and helped when needed. He felt he needed to support Michelle now. He recognized how fragile she was when she was hospitalized.

Angela asked, "So, have y'all ordered a cake, or do we need to do that?"

"I think my father asked my aunt to take care of it."

Angela knew Linda was helping with meals and keeping up the wash. Life goes on, even if you have a void that needs to be filled.

"Okay, please just drop me off at home instead. I need to do a few things before tomorrow."

"All right, if you're sure," said Brent.

Angela had been working on a painting for Michelle. She took drawing lessons during the school year and got pretty good at doing charcoal drawings. Her picture was of Michelle, Lisa, and Linda's backs as they stood on their front porch and looked out toward the yard. It was almost finished, but she wanted to add some personal touches. She hoped Michelle would like it and not upset her too much.

She kissed Brent and told him to stay in the truck. She reminded him to hide the gift or leave it in the truck. He smiled at the reminder and watched her walk into the house. He thought *there goes my future wife*. He put the truck in reverse and backed out of the gravel drive. On his way home, he reflected on the last two weeks and all that had happened to his family. He was smart enough to know that most families didn't survive well when this kind of tragedy occurred. There was usually a divorce. There was guilt and suspicions. He just wished he knew where Lisa was and that she was alive.

"Mom, I'm home," said Angela as she walked in. Andy ran up and hugged her around the waist. "Hi, little brother, where's mom?"

"She went to borrow some sugar."

Angela looked at the time on the wall clock: one-thirty-five. She went to her room, got her drawing, and took it into the living room with her pencils. She showed the picture to Andy, and he approved it with confidence. She added some flower pots and butterflies along the edges to give it more life.

Before she knew it, she looked up, and it was two-twenty. Andy would have been alone for over an hour or more if she had not come home. He couldn't say when she left. She was getting very antsy about the situation.

She asked Andy, "Which neighbor?" but he said he didn't know. He pointed to the right side like she had gone to the right-side neighbor. She went out on the porch and looked both ways but saw no one. Then, when she turned around, she saw her mother coming out of the house across the street. She wasn't carrying anything in her hands, and the neighbor she visited was standing in the doorway with his boxer shorts on.

Angela started walking toward her, and when her mom looked up, she looked startled to see her. "Where have you been for the last hour or more?" Angela asked her.

"I'm sorry. I went next door to borrow sugar, but they were not home, so I went across the street, and Phil was home. We got to talking, and time got away from me."

Angela knew her mother was doing more than just talking because her hair was messed up, and she looked disheveled. "Look, mother. If you want to see this man, please don't do it when you have to leave Andy alone. You know better than that!"

Her mother sheepishly said, "I know, I messed up. But we get along so well and like each other's company."

Angela stared at her, turned, and returned to their house. They didn't speak for the rest of the afternoon. Her mother left for work at four o'clock, leaving Angela to feed Andy and care for him, but she didn't mind.

Angela finished the picture she was planning to give Michelle for her birthday. She was pleased with it. She had already purchased a black frame. Once secured, she again showed it to Andy, and he gave it a thumbs up. After finding a box large enough for it, she looked in her mother's closet for birthday paper or a bag she could use. Her mom kept all of it on a top shelf in her closet. She found a pink bag and some white ribbon, which was perfect. She planned to pick up a card tomorrow morning. Her mother was taking her and Andy to Walmart to go grocery shopping. Hopefully, they will have made up and be on speaking terms by then. It should be fun and interesting. Her mother was still on a nutritious food kick. Angela was surprised she had kept it up this long. She had to admit that they were eating better.

She thought Andy's father had something to do with it. She overheard her mother on the phone with him and kept saying, I know, I know. Angela was sure Keith was telling her he was sending extra money because the economy was in the tank and things were more expensive, and he expected her to use it to buy the kids better food without preservatives. She saw her mother's deposit slip the last time she went to the bank. It was $500 more than usual. Angela had gotten used to seeing and hearing the tells. She was very mature for her age and knew she had to be to survive and help raise Andy.

chapter

44

Vera was getting sleepy while Gil was driving toward Wilmington. She checked on Lisa about an hour ago and found her in the same position. She didn't appear to be waking up, so she held off on the Phenergan but gave her another dose of Valium to make sure she would not move to get out. Her best way to keep her loose was to keep her muscles flaccid. She didn't like trying to play chemist and nurse. She hoped they would be there soon and the transfer could take place.

"How much longer, Gil?"

"According to the GPS, less than forty-five minutes. I know you are tired. You have had a lot to deal with. Try to rest; it's almost over. I'll make a great payday on this one. We'll go on a vacation, well deserved."

Vera smiled at him and leaned the seat back. The car's bright lights kept her from sleeping, but she was trying to rest her eyes. All of a sudden, she heard a scream. She looked behind them in the truck bed and saw the crate shaking. Lisa was awake and freaking out. "Stop the car. I've got to check on our passenger!"

Gil put his blinker on and slowly pulled off to the side of the road. He looked behind him and saw Jeffrey do the same. Vera started drawing up Phenergan in a syringe. She would need help holding her to give her the injection. She and Gil got out of the truck. It was very dangerous, and they wanted to get it done quickly. Jeffrey exited his car as well and came to assist. Vera climbed into the bed and opened the crate to reach her hip easier. She heard Lisa screaming very loudly, which didn't help her nerves. Now, she wished she'd drawn the Valium, too. She gave her the injection and asked Gil to get her kit on the front seat. He brought it to her, and, using the same syringe, after wiping the top with alcohol, she drew up Valium and gave her another shot. The Valium will work quickly.

Jeffrey said, "Let's return to the road and get off at the next exit. We're too exposed here. We don't need the Highway Patrol stopping to see what was happening."

Gil agreed, so he and Vera hopped back into the cab and got back on the highway. There was an exit about a mile ahead, so they both exited again. It had a truck stop, so Gil pulled in. He stopped, turned the car off, and he and Vera got out to check on Lisa. Vera again got in the truck bed, checked her breathing and pulse, and announced that she was asleep.

"Great, let's keep going; not much farther, said Jeffrey. Gil agreed.

When Jeffrey returned to his car, he called Cobbler on the SAT phone, and he immediately picked up. "Hi, there. Is everything okay?"

"We just had a scare with our girl, but we believe it's under control. When will you be in Wilmington?" asked Jeffrey.

"Change of plans. There's a risk of detection. I have been monitoring the situation all day, and I've been warned of a possible sting operation out of Wilmington. Our next stop is going to have to be Charleston. I am sorry."

"What? That wasn't how we planned it. If I had known that, I would have taken the yacht. This is turning into a shit show, pardon my French," said Jeffrey.

"It'll be okay. Charleston isn't that far of a drive from Wilmington."

"It's at least three hours. The people transporting her have her in a fruit transport crate with blankets for warmth. They were keeping her sedated, but it was risky. The woman's a retired nurse who's good with the dosages. They won't be happy about the change of plans one bit. Let me call them. Text me the details about Charleston. I'll probably be calling you back."

chapter

45

Eliza and Jay saw no action around Jeffrey's yacht at the marina. The marina captain had told them he hadn't returned as far as he knew. They waited until noon and called Sheriff Taylor.

"I don't think he's going to show. He must have another mode of transportation. We are ready to give it up and come back to Murphy. Is anything going on there?" asked Eliza.

"Just the usual. We are still working on the tips that have come in, but they aren't promising. Did you guys ever figure out what car he was driving?" asked Kellum.

"We assumed he rented a car at the airport where he left his car. Do you have any reason to believe anything else?"

"How about I get Judge Casey to give me a warrant to go to the rental car agents and see if they rented him a car? I'll start at the closest rental agency to his car's location. Ask Jay to send me the information on his app so I can find his car."

"He's sending a screenshot to you now," said Eliza.

"Great. See you guys when you get here."

Sheriff Taylor had a call on his other line. It was James Sisk from Martin Curtis's law firm. "Good afternoon, Sheriff. I will be coming over to see you shortly, and it is a matter of urgency, but I will need to protect my client, Walter Green. Is it safe to come to you now? He's ready to confess to assisting in the abduction of Lisa Williams."

"Did I hear you correctly? Is he going to confess to the kidnapping? Does he know where she is? We need to get to her as soon as possible."

"No, he doesn't know where she is now, but he can give you some information to help search."

"Okay, please come right away. I'll be waiting."

"His wife, Sandy, will be with us."

"Got it. See you shortly."

Kellum called Eliza's phone, and when she answered, he told her, "Get here as fast as you can. We have one of the abductors coming to turn himself in."

"Who?" asked Eliza.

"Walter Green," said Kellum.

"Does he know where she is?"

"Not exactly," Kellum told her.

Eliza hung up and told Jay what Sheriff Taylor told her. "I knew it," said Jay.

Jay put the siren on the dashboard, and Eliza pushed the limits to get them there in record time.

In the meantime, Jay contacted his boss and told him of the new developments. They were on their way in to interview Walter Green. "I feel strongly that Jeffrey Edwards needs to be leaned on. I'll need a warrant to search his house."

"Working on it now. I'll call you as soon as possible," said his boss. Jay knew he meant it.

Chief Agent Rosen had no place in his heart for child kidnappers. Jay heard all of the stories about Agent Rosen being a victim of a child abductor when he was very young. Fortunately, he had a mom who immediately started screaming and running after the woman until she turned Alex loose. She miscalculated the kidnapping; so many people had seen it, and the mall security caught her quickly while she headed for her car. It was in broad daylight, thankfully. Agent Rosen had told that story to classes of agents whenever he was asked to speak.

He was traumatized by the event, and even though his parents got him therapy, it only made him crawl further into his shell. The Bureau was what helped him the most. He decided to be in the FBI at a young age, particularly in the kidnapping division. Ever since the Lindbergh baby kidnapping in the 1930s, the FBI had a child kidnapping division, and they have jurisdiction in every state.

chapter

46

J effrey called Gil after he had finished talking with Cobbler. "I've got some bad news," he said.

"What?" asked Gil. Vera looked over at Gil with a quizzical stare.

"The ship won't be able to enter the Wilmington port. They got a tip that it would be too dangerous because law enforcement checked everything everywhere. We may have stirred a beehive."

"We?" asked Gil sarcastically.

"Get off at the next exit and pull to the field down the road on the right so we can talk. I don't want anyone seeing us."

Gil drove out on the road, turning right away from the highway. "Where are you going?" asked Vera.

"Jeffrey needs to talk with us about something."

After he pulled off into the field, Jeffrey pulled up behind them. They all got out of the car.

"What's up?" asked Gil. Vera was at his side. She had looked into the truck's bed and had heard nothing from their passenger.

"We've got to go to Charleston. I am sorry, but she needs to be unloaded in a different port where they are less secure. Many yachts go in and out of there regularly, so another one won't be noticed. My contact just called and said Wilmington was too dangerous. He had heard from his sources that Wilmington was being watched, and there was more law enforcement around than usual."

He looked at Vera to see what her reaction would be.

Vera screamed at Jeffrey, "I am not going to Charleston; this is all too much. I am done." She looked at Gil for support.

"I have to agree with Vera," he told Jeffrey; the girl has to be medicated so often, and I don't want to drive any farther. You are looking at another three or four hours. I say we cut our losses and run."

Jeffrey suddenly pulled a gun out of his coat pocket and pointed it at Vera. "Now look here, you are not calling the shots. I am. Get back in the car and start driving."

Vera said, "What are you going to do, kill all of us?"

"I will if I have to," and he pointed the gun at Vera's chest.

Gil moved to his left to shield Vera, but Jeffrey pulled the trigger and hit Gil in his thigh. Vera screamed and started running away into the field. Jeffrey pointed the gun at her and pulled the trigger, and she fell forward.

Gil was writhing in pain and screaming for Vera. At that moment, they both heard Lisa screaming and cursing, "Get me out of here, you son of a bitch. I'll kill you!"

Jeffrey threw the gun away from Vera as far out in the field as possible. He then ran and jumped in his car, and took off.

Gil managed to pull out his cell phone and dialed 911.

"What is your emergency," the voice asked. "I've been shot. My wife has been shot."

"Sir, tell me where you are so I can help."

"We are next to the Pilot Station near Wallace off Hwy 84. That's all I know," he got out between gasping for breaths.

"An ambulance is on the way, sir, but stay on the phone with me so I don't lose you; please keep talking. What is your name and your wife's name? Do you know if your wife is alive?"

"I am not sure, but I pray she is," he told her. My name is Gil Whitlock, and my wife's name is Vera. "Another thing, we have that girl that was abducted in Blaylock County, Lisa Williams."

"Okay, sir, I am writing all of this down. Can you tell me if the girl is alive?"

"Oh, yes, she is very much alive," Gil chuckled as he could hear Lisa still screaming and kicking.

The 911 operator kept him talking about anything until he told her he could hear the ambulance. The 911 operator could hear the sirens through the phone, which was getting louder and louder. "I think they have found you, am I right?"

"Yes, they are pulling in now; thank you so much for saving us," he started crying as he laid the phone beside him.

"I have a live one here," said the officer. There was a helicopter hovering over the area, looking for a shooter or other victims.

"There appears to be a body face down about two hundred yards to your south," said the helicopter pilot into Sgt. Hibbard's ear. Sgt. Hibbard started walking using his flashlight away from where the other victim was being treated, and he found a woman fully clothed lying prone in the grass. He felt her carotid artery, but there appeared to be no pulse. Then he tried to get her to respond, but he knew she was dead.

He returned to the scene where the paramedics were working on the man, but before he could say anything, a girl screamed, "I'm over here."

He approached the truck and saw what looked like a large shipping crate, but it had blankets, like the kind you use for moving, stuffed on the inside all around it. He could hear the faint cries of a girl saying, "I'm here, I'm here."

He jumped into the bed of the truck and opened the top by prying it apart using the butt of his flashlight like a hammer. Once enough of it cracked, he lifted it off quite easily. He unraveled the blankets and found a young girl curled up.

She was warm but barely responsive. He yelled to the paramedics to get up in the truck and help him. Three gently lifted Lisa Williams from her makeshift transportable shipping container and placed her onto a gurney. The paramedics began working on her, trying to stimulate her to respond, but it was not working. She had slipped into unresponsiveness. They loaded her into the ambulance. Luckily, another ambulance had just pulled up to get the other person.

When the paramedic got Lisa in the ambulance, he started an IV and infused normal saline fluid. She was obviously dehydrated. They didn't see any apparent wounds. They wouldn't know if she had been sexually assaulted until they arrived at the hospital and she had a thorough exam. They were headed to Pender's emergency room, but chances were good that a medic helicopter would be there to transport her to Children's Hospital.

Meanwhile, the Pender County sheriff had arrived and put handcuffs on Gil. There had been a warrant put out for his arrest on suspicion of kidnapping. Gil sustained a right thigh wound that barely missed his femoral artery, or he would be dead. The first responders had done an excellent job of quickly assessing him for other wounds and even drugs or weapons. Fortunately for him, they found none. He had been given a painkiller and was now knocked out while being prepared for transport. He didn't yet know the fate of his wife.

The county coroner had been summoned and was there within the hour. Vera was lifted onto another gurney with a body bag and transported to the Pender County morgue. The coroner will have to make a next-of-kin notification. It will probably be to Gil once he awakens at the Pender County hospital.

Detective Rex Harrison arrived at the same time as the coroner. He walked over and said, "Sam, what on earth happened here?"

"Your guess is as good as mine. Besides, that's why they pay you the big bucks," he chuckled.

Detective Harrison called over to the officers on the scene, "Have you found a weapon, shell casings?"

"We did find shell casings and may find more in the morning when we have light. No gun yet. It looks like it could be a .22."

"Let's fan out in all directions, just in case the perpetrator threw it. It probably wouldn't have gone too far."

The three started walking out from the scene and doing essential back-and-forth moves about two hundred yards out. After about ten minutes, Officer Hernandez called out that he found a gun. Rex walked over and looked down at it, "Yep, looks like a .22. " He pulled out a pair of gloves and picked it up, using his pen inserted in the barrel to avoid disturbing prints. They walked back to his car, and he put the gun in an evidence bag and sealed it. Then he pulled out a paper sleeve and opened it, and the other officer put the casings in. There were three of them. "I think we have all of the casings. We'll know after the bodies are examined."

"Thanks, I think we can go home. Did anyone call for transport of the truck?"

Officer Hernandez said, "Yes, but they were already on a run, so it may be a while."

"Okay, sorry, but you two will have to wait."

Detective Harrison called the officer who went with their prisoner. "Sir?" he answered.

"Jake, make sure his hands are bagged; we need to check for gunpowder residue. The son of a bitch may have shot his wife and himself. Has he said anything yet?"

"No sir, still knocked out from the morphine."

"Good. Make sure to call me when he wakes up. I want a statement from him ASAP."

"Copy that," said Officer Jake Tapper.

chapter 47

James Sisk opened the Sheriff's door for Walter and Sandy Green. Sheriff Taylor was waiting and led them into an interrogation room.

Kellum sat down, put the tape in the machine on the table, and told them this interrogation would be recorded. They nodded their understanding. Kellum saw Sisk's grin as he put the tape in and said, "We do things the old-fashioned way, with a small budget."

After pressing the buttons to record, Kellum said, "Today is Friday, June 30th, and the time is eight-fifteen p.m. Walter Green is here with his wife, intending to give a statement relating to the kidnapping of Lisa Williams. Would you state your name, Mr. Green?"

"Yes, sir. I'm Walter Green, and I willingly assisted with the kidnapping of Lisa Williams. I'm here to turn myself in and be of any help I can to find Ms. Williams. I don't know where she is right now."

For the next thirty minutes, with his lawyer's help, Walter told precisely how they kidnapped her and admitted she was targeted.

In the middle of the confession, Eliza and Jay got to the station and entered the room. They both introduced themselves, and the first thing out of Eliza's mouth was, "Did Jeffrey Edwards have anything to do with her kidnapping?"

"Yes, it was his idea. I went along with it because Vinnie asked me to help. He was the one that picked her out and orchestrated everything."

Kellum's cell phone rang, and he looked at the number. He did not recognize it but answered it anyway and heard, "We have her."

"Who is this?" asked Kellum.

"This is Sheriff Brad Prince of Pender County."

"I'm going to put you on speakerphone. Is that okay?" Kellum asked Sheriff Prince.

"Fine by me. She has been taken to Pender County ER for evaluation, and they are getting her ready to be airlifted to Children's Hospital in Raleigh. I wanted to give you the good news."

"Any details, like how, where, etc."

"I can tell you she was in the back of an F150 in a large produce-type crate with many blankets. One of the perpetrators is in custody but has a leg wound from a gunshot, so he is in Pender County Hospital. His accomplice was shot and killed, a woman named Vera Gardner, according to the ID in her purse. His name is Gil Gardner, so I assumed they were married. The 911 operator told us that he said he and his wife had been shot. So that you know, he has not yet been told that his wife was killed. He was knocked out with pain medications while being transported.

"That is great news. Is the girl okay?"

"As far as I know, she will be fine. Not sure of any sexual trauma. Leave that to the experts."

"Sheriff, this is Eliza Mancini with the FBI. Do you know if Jeffrey Edwards was at the scene?"

"Don't know that for sure, but whoever shot those two people fled the scene. We found the gun, so we will be forensically processing it along with the shell casings. Mr. Gardner went into surgery as soon as he arrived at the hospital, so we will have that bullet soon. I will check with the coroner tomorrow about the woman's bullet. She will probably be sent to Fayetteville for the autopsy. That is usually the process down here."

"Thank you, Sheriff, for the notification. My detective will be down first thing in the morning to see Mr. Gardner. Now we have to find our main perpetrator, Jeffrey Edwards."

Eliza and Jay told Kellum they would now go to the Edwards house. "You have a search warrant, right?" asked Jay.

"Yes, all signed and ready," said Kellum.   "Let's go," said Jay.

Kellum continued interrogating Walter. "When did you and Vinnie get rid of Lisa, and to whom?"

"Two guys came to the house we used. They had a van and backed up into the carport. We had given her medication, so she was limp, and Vinnie helped them take her upstairs and put her in their van. She had injured me by using a fork left after she kicked her plate of food. I foolishly didn't find all of the utensils. I was icing my eye when that transport took place. They came to get her Saturday night around nine, I believe."

"What were their names?" asked Kellum.

"I never saw them and didn't ask Vinnie. I believe he said they were brothers, but who knows if that was true?" said Walter.

"Where is Vinnie?"

"I think he may have gone home to New York. I haven't seen him for a week. He has a brother or two up there, and he was going to stay with them, and no, I have no idea where it is."

"What's Vinnie's last name?"

"I don't know. We only used first names."

James Sisk said, "I think that's enough questions for today. Where do we go from here, like I don't know."

"Stand up, Walter. You are under arrest for the kidnapping of Lisa Williams and any other crimes that were connected." He read him his Miranda rights, and they allowed him to hug Sandy and then took him back for processing.

"Sandy, he will go before the magistrate on Monday morning, and bail will probably be set, but it is up to the magistrate. Will that give you time to get things in order?" asked Kellum.

"Yes, sir. I will be able to be there on Monday. I should be able to handle the bail by putting our house up. James will walk me through it. That's why I hired him."

chapter

48

Jay and Eliza raced to the Edwards' home. After ringing the doorbell, Stella Edwards appeared. They barged in and showed her the search warrant.

"What is going on?"

"Your husband is a prime suspect in the kidnapping of Lisa Williams, and we need to know where he is. You could be arrested as an accessory if you do not cooperate. Where is he?"

The technicians arrived with them and gathered every computer and phone they could find in the home. Stella, wearing a loose white blouse and black Lululemon yoga pants, stood in a state of shock and literally could not say anything.

Finally, she got her voice and said to Eliza, "Jeffrey hasn't been home for three days. I've tried calling him on his cell phone, but it goes straight to voice mail."

"What kind of car is he driving?"

"What do you mean?" asked Stella.

"We know he left his car at the airport and rented a car about a week ago. You see, we had a tracker on the Mercedes and noticed a few days ago that it had been stationary at the airport, so the conclusion was that he must have rented a car."

"But why would he do that?" She thought it was insensitive of Jeffrey to lie to her about the car in the shop.

"It's obvious he's trying to avoid us. He had an active role in the kidnapping and probable transfer for purposes of the sex trafficking of Lisa Williams. Turn around and put your hands behind your back, Eliza told Stella Edwards. We are taking you in as an accessory but more for your protection. Do you understand?"

"Yyyyess, I think so," she stuttered.

"Your husband is wanted for an attempted murder and a murder in cold blood. He is a dangerous man. Also, does he own a .22?"

"I don't think so, but I do."

"Where is it?"

"We keep them in the main bedroom closet safe."

"Okay, take me to it," demanded Eliza. Jay followed Eliza's lead and proceeded up the stairs.

They went to the master bedroom, and one of the techs opened it after Stella gave him the code 0812, "our wedding date," she murmured demurely.

Jay looked inside, "There isn't a .22 in here, but there is a .45 and what looks to be a pistol, probably from one of the wars. Many men brought them home; my grandfather did," he mused.

"Okay, we can take Mrs. Williams to the station to finish question-ing her. Tell the techs to lock up when they finish their job."

"Done. Let's go," said Jay.

Stella didn't like leaving her home, especially in a police car. *What will the neighbors think?* She thought to herself.

On the way to the police station, Jay called Sheriff Taylor, and when he answered, Jay said, "We are bringing Mrs. Edwards in; there is no sign of Jeffrey. My guess is he has headed for his yacht."

From the back seat, Stella said, "It's my yacht."

Jay asked, "Do you have access to a helicopter? It would take too long to drive to the marina."

Sheriff Taylor said, "Max Sheridan, a friend of Trent's, came in a week ago and told me to contact him if we need anything. He mentioned that he has a helicopter and he flies it himself. I will call him now and have your answer when you arrive."

"Thank you, Sheriff."

Kellum called the number Max had given him. He had it on the calendar on his desk and was glad he could find it so quickly. Max answered on the first ring. When Kellum told him what he needed, he said, "Tell them to meet me at the Blaylock Airport, and I will have it ready."

"Thank you so much," said Kellum. He knew it was time to get over to the Williams' home. It would be good news this time, and he wanted to deliver it in person.

When Jay hung up the phone, he smiled as he told Eliza they were going by helicopter to the marina. He explained to her what Sheriff Taylor said about having a friend of Trent's who had offered his services.

When he said the name, Stella said, "That is wonderful news. I know who Max is; his wife and I went to college together. They are a wonderful family. I hope you find Jeffrey. I have a few things I would like to ask him."

They rode the rest of the way in silence. Jay and Eliza were coming off a high about learning Lisa was safe. But they knew the work had just begun. Finding Jeffrey Edwards was their primary goal now.

chapter

49

Sheriff Taylor drove to the Williams' house by himself. He told Todd to stay at the station if anything else was needed. "The parts are moving so fast, I can barely keep up," he informed him.

When he drove up, Michelle saw the police car from the upper window. She was still awake and was sitting in Lisa's room. It was almost eleven, and the house lights were off. Kellum saw all the front lights come on as he walked up the steps. Michelle opened the door and looked strained, but Kellum smiled and said, "We got her, and she's safe."

Michelle went to her knees. Trent, Brent, and Linda were running down the steps from their respective bedrooms. Michelle was crying, but Trent saw Kellum's smile and knew she was weeping tears of joy.

Trent spoke first. "Come in, Sheriff. Let's all go into the living room." He helped Michelle to her feet. Brent and Linda were jumping up and down.

Kellum said, "She is being transported to Children's Hospital, but they tell me it's just precautionary. She should be there soon, but you know how things move, never as fast as you would like."

Trent asked, "Where was she found?"

"Well, that's the thing. It was in the back of a pickup truck in a large crate. She was unconscious when they found her, but the paramedics started IVs and gave her fluids while she was being transported to the first hospital. It was in Pender County."

"Who had her?" asked Brent.

"I don't have all of the details right now. But I can share that one of the kidnappers was found dead. It was a woman. The other one, her husband, we believe, was wounded by a gunshot."

Michelle gasped.

"The woman had been shot in the back, probably because she was running away, we don't know."

"Who shot them?" asked Michelle.

"Another good question. We think Jeffrey Edwards, the billionaire hedge fund guy we have been watching, is our prime suspect. The FBI is getting ready to board a helicopter flown by your friend, Max Sheridan."

Trent's eyes got as wide as saucers, and he said, "Really, well, I'll be darn. How did you know to call him?"

"He came into the sheriff's office about a week ago and offered his services. What do you know? We needed him. He's flying Agents Camp and Mancini to the marina in New Bern, where Jeffrey Edwards keeps his yacht."

"When can we see our daughter?" Michelle asked.

"Just as soon as possible, get ready and drive to the hospital. I'll arrange a police escort," offered Kellum, smiling as broadly as he could.

While the Williams were getting ready, Kellum called Todd and asked him to contact Evan at home and ask him to get over to the Williams's home. He said, "They will see their daughter tonight, and I want to give them a police escort."

"Yes, sir," said Todd.

Next, Kellum called Sabrina Johnson on her cell and gave her the scoop. She had always favored the work of the local police, and he felt she deserved the first call. "Hello, Sheriff."

"You're up late," he said to her.

"Crime news never sleeps," she retorted.

"Well, there is good news on Lisa Williams: she has been found alive. I will hold a news conference in front of the sheriff's office at ten o'clock in the morning. I would appreciate you being there. I am letting you know first. The news will break during the night. It involves another jurisdiction, and we are not getting all the facts."

"Thank you, Sheriff. I will be there with bells on my toes. In fact, I will drive to the news station now to get things organized. That is great news."

"Yes, it is."

He didn't want to give her Lisa's location until her family had seen her. He knew the media would hunt her down, but he didn't want to be the source they used.

He next called his wife and gave Shannon the great news. She had a lot of questions, but he told her he would tell her everything when he got home. He drove back to the station, and when he learned that Eliza and Jay had already left for the airport, he decided to go home and sleep for a couple of hours. He knew he wouldn't sleep much; Shannon would have to be sated with answers, and he needed a shower and change of clothes in the worst way.

❀ ❀ ❀

When Trent, Michelle, Linda, and Brent entered the Children's Hospital front door, it was a relief; Michelle started crying again. They walked to the reception area, and a lovely lady looked up and said, "I think I know who you are here to see."

She got up, came around her desk, hugged Michelle, and shook Trent's hand. She nodded to both of their children and said, "Follow me."

They walked toward the Emergency Room, and a doctor came to greet them when they arrived.

"I am Dr. Sullivan, and I will happily take you to your daughter."

Trent noted that no one had even asked their names. He wondered if Sheriff Taylor called ahead to let them know they were on their way.

Dr. Sullivan took them to a private conference room first. They all sat down. They looked at each other, wondering why he would first take them to a conference room. Michelle almost broke down again. Her thoughts were that Lisa had passed away.

Dr. Sullivan spoke. "I wanted to have a word with you before you saw Lisa. She is perfectly fine. I performed an examination and didn't note any wounds or bruising. She refused a vaginal exam. I'm sorry to be so blunt, but of course, the police would want to know if she had been sexually assaulted. She promised me that she had not."

Michelle realized she was holding her breath and let out a long sigh.

"Is it ok for us to see her now?" asked Trent.

"It is, yes. I would try not to ask her too many questions. Let her gradually tell you what she went through in her time. Trauma is tricky, particularly in children. She is in a good place, and the police in Pender are smart enough to move her immediately. They should be commended. We have a social worker in the department who has met with her, and she will help you navigate any issue that may come up. Please let me know if there is anything else I can do to help. She is in good hands."

"Yes, sir," they each mumbled.

"Come with me." He got up and held the door open for them.

They followed him to bay fourteen. The curtain was pulled for privacy, so he peeked in and saw she was awake. "Lisa, your family is here."

Lisa said, "Please let them in. I want my mother!"

Michelle went first, Lisa sat up in bed, and they hugged for a long time. Lisa was crying, as was Michelle. Then they both started laughing, and they all began screaming and laughing simultaneously, tears flowing.

Trent went over, put his hand on her head, and said, "My sweet little girl, you don't know how much we've missed and prayed for you." He started breaking down, and Michelle went over and pulled him away. They hugged each other. Lisa noticed it and felt so bad for them.

"Mom, Dad, I have missed you so much, and I want you to know that I had a lot of time to think, and I know I have been a rotten kid and even a bitch at times; yes, I said it, but it is true. I hope you will forgive me."

Michelle broke away from Trent, kissed Lisa on her cheek, and said you are not a bitch, not my child, never. We love you and always will."

Brent and Linda went to her and hugged and kissed her. Brent said, "I think you should clean our rooms for the next month for all of the heartache you put us through." He winked at her and said, "Just kidding, sis. We love you and are so glad you are back with us. Don't ever leave again."

At that, they all started crying and laughing again.

The curtain was pulled slightly back, and a woman with long dark hair held in place with a headband said, "I see you all are having a grand time. I just wanted to introduce myself to your family, Lisa. I am Nancy Williams, and I have no apparent relation to you, but I wish I did because you seem like such a wonderful family. I am Lisa's social worker, and she and I have talked. I wanted you to know you have a remarkable daughter. If there is anything you need, don't hesitate to ask. Here is my card." She handed Michelle her card and left the room.

Lisa said, "She is nice." She then looked at her father and stated, "I think I would like to be a social worker when I grow up."

They all started laughing and nodding their approval.

chapter
50

When Kellum was driving home, he called the Raleigh police department and spoke with the Commander. He requested that they put an officer at Lisa Williams' room door at the Children's Hospital. "Do you mean the girl that was abducted in Blaylock County?" asked Lt. Sanders.

"The one and the same."

"Absolutely. On it."

Kellum then called Trent on his cell phone and told him they were putting an officer on her at the hospital. Trent told him he appreciated it, and they had just had a great visit with her and were on their way home. He said they were pumped up on adrenaline but now were coming down and getting tired. Kellum told him he would call him tomorrow...meaning today. "I am having a news conference at ten o'clock this morning. Just in case one or all of you would like to be there, but it's not required, there will be a chance later if you want to make a statement."

"Thanks for letting me know, but I think we will be too exhausted to make it. Thank everyone for us, please."

"Yes, of course," Kellum told him.

He then contacted the New Bern police chief and asked for backup to be sent to the airport. "There is a helicopter coming in with two FBI agents, and they are going to the marina to confront a suspect in a shooting in Pender County."

"Is that the same one where they found the girl that had been kidnapped?"

"Yes, sir. I am afraid so. The prime suspect owns a yacht and keeps it in New Bern. His name is Jeffrey Edwards. Do you know him?"

"I know the name. We have a log of the boats so I can find where he is docked. I'll get my officers to head out there now. Do you think they have landed by now because they could be on their way to the marina?"

"I don't think they would have landed yet. Can you call there to find out?"

"Yes, I can do that. We've got you covered. Try and get some rest."

"Thank you."

At two a.m., Eliza and Jay got out of the helicopter. The police car was waiting for them.

They thanked Max repeatedly for helping out. He told them he had family in the area, and they were coming to pick him up so he wouldn't have to fly back tonight. "Best of luck to both of you. Please be safe," he told them.

Officer Dan Cooper drove them to the marina. They remembered where it was, but the officer had it pulled up on his screen.

"Do you think he is there?" asked Officer Cooper.

"We hope so, but we wouldn't be surprised if he weren't," said Jay.

As soon as they drove up, Jay took Officer Cooper's binoculars and could see that the yacht was missing.

"He's in the wind. I'll call it in."

Officer Cooper drove them back to the station. Each took an available cell and tried to get some shut-eye until daylight hit, which wasn't that long. After bad coffee, Jay asked for a ride to the closest car rental.

They tried to analyze what they had on the drive back to Murray.

"Okay, we know Walter was the one in the bathroom, but he only knows Vinnie's first name, he says." Eliza rolled her eyes as she said this.

"We need to get to the hospital as soon as possible to interview Lisa. I got a text from Sheriff Taylor about him putting an officer on her door."

"Yes, I was on that same text."

"That's right. I remember that now. I am beyond tired, but there is work to be done."

"We need to know the address from Vera's driver's license. That's it! She was probably kept in their home before being transferred."

"You're right. I am calling the Pender police department right now to track that down. If they don't have it, we should be able to get Gil's driver's license from the hospital. Better yet, I will call Sheriff Taylor and have him get in the DMV records—quicker than anything else."

Kellum answered on the first ring. "Sheriff, we need the address for Gil and Vera Whitlock as soon as possible. Jeffrey Edwards' yacht is gone. We wanted to go to their house and see if that was where they kept Lisa. As for Jeffrey Edwards, he is in the wind. We need an all-points bulletin for him, including the Coast Guard. The name of the Yacht is The Sophie Marie."

"I'll be back as soon as I get the address and get on the other requests, too. See you back at the station at some point. When will y'all be able to interview Lisa?" asked Kellum.

"I don't know right now, so keep the officer on the door and don't let anyone else near her except for family."

Sheriff Taylor called Agent Camp a few minutes later with their address: "It's not in Blaylock County. It's Morgan Pass in Ross County. The house number is 8720. It is a rural area, which I suspected. Ross is not very populated. Be careful; people are suspicious in those areas."

"Advice noted. Thanks."

Jay put the address in his Google Maps and found it. "He's right, very rural. My guess is this is definitely where they kept her."

He put the siren on the dash, and Eliza took off like lightning. Within the hour, they were driving up to the Whitlock property.

When they got out of the car, they found an ASICS running shoe. Eliza picked it up and showed Jay. "I kind of doubt Vera or Gil were runners." She placed the shoe in an evidence bag. They pulled their weapons, and after knocking and getting no response, Jay kicked in the front door; they entered and searched the house and, as expected, found no one there. Next, they saw the room where Lisa had been kept. There was a single bed with the sheets disheveled and a potty chair next to the bed. Eliza checked the potty chair, but it was cleaned out. It's too bad it's immediate DNA, but the CSI unit may get something from it.

They left by the front door, and Jay called the Ross Co. Sheriff's Department and requested they bring the CSI unit over there. The Sheriff got on the phone, and Jay told him where they were. The Sheriff said Sheriff Taylor had already called to inform him we would probably be calling. "We'll have the team out there within the hour."

"Do you think you could send an Officer now so we can get back to Blaylock Co.? We have a lot to check up on there."

"Sure thing. They are leaving now. It will only be about ten minutes."

True to his word, two officers pulled up about ten minutes later. They briefed them on what was happening, returned to their rental, and headed to the Blaylock station.

On the way, they received a call from Sheriff Taylor telling them that Gil Whitlock was being transported back to Blaylock County tomorrow. "He had surgery on his thigh to remove the bullet, and he is stable enough to travel in a car.

Detective Mason Henry will be with him. Pender County is sending him in one of their cars with two officers. He will be well-guarded."

"That's great news, Sheriff. Has he made a statement yet?" asked Jay.

"He has, and I have it here. I know both of you will want to interrogate him as well. This is a tri-county investigation."

"FBI will take over now. I'm sure you understand. It is a real hot mess," said Jay.

"Yes, it is. See you in a little while."

chapter

51

Agents Mancini and Camp arrived at the station at one o'clock. On the way, they did a quick drive-through at a Chick-fil-A. Eliza noted the irony in that Lisa was taken from the mall near Chick-fil-A.

"We started near a Chick-fil-A, and we are almost at the end and back at a Chick-fil-A. Ironic, huh?"

"Agree, we are not nearly done, but we are progressing. Do you want to take Lisa and I'll interview Mrs. Edwards? Divide and conquer?"

"Sounds good. You wouldn't want to interview Mrs. Edwards because she is so beautiful and about to become a divorcee. I am just speculating. I would divorce that SOB if I were her. No standing by my man crap," said Eliza.

Jay laughed, "You were reading my mind, Eliza. I never told you my background, and being the polite person you are, you never asked."

"So, what is your story? I did notice you didn't wear a wedding band, but a lot of men don't, so that doesn't mean anything."

"I was engaged a very long time ago. My fiancé was one of the victims of 9/11," Jay told her.

"No, really? Oh my gosh, I am so sorry," said Eliza.

"Yes, so am I. She was a wonderful person. We met in law school at Columbia and planned to marry after graduation. She worked for a law firm in the South Tower. She never made a call, so I don't have her voice recorded like many others did from their loved ones. I wish I did. I had a habit of deleting voicemails quickly.

Back then, the flip phones didn't have as much storage capacity as now."

"It's been so long. You never found anyone else, huh?"

"No, I haven't, but it's my own fault. I work all the time, much more than is good for me, but I love it. I don't golf or do any other sports. I love to read and collect several books from my favorite authors. I enjoy spy novels and, of course, anything to do with the FBI. I can relate and be a critic at the same time."

"Have you thought of putting yourself out there as a consultant?"

"No, but that is a thought. I may look into doing that when I retire, but that is a while."

Sheriff Taylor briefed them on what was happening when they arrived at the station.

"We believe there was a third place Lisa was kept, perhaps just for a short time. She told her mother she was moved twice after the first place. She was more awake and coherent in the last place but was still having trouble remembering due to the drugs they gave her. The hospital in Pender did a drug test and found Valium in her system at a high level."

Eliza left to go to the hospital to see Lisa. When she arrived, the officer was still stationed at the door. She made a mental note to check with Sheriff Taylor to see if it was still necessary. They have their main suspects, and she doesn't think Jeffrey Edwards will be showing up here.

Lisa was alone, sitting in bed, wearing shorts and a simple white sleeveless shirt. Her long blond hair had been brushed and looked recently washed. She didn't have an IV running now but still had a port in her wrist. A doll beside her had a pretty blue dress and blond hair like hers.

"Hi, Lisa. You don't know me, but I have been hoping to meet you in the worst way," she chuckled. "How are you feeling?"

Lisa smiled, "I feel great and am ready to go home. I showered this morning and ate a great breakfast: pancakes and bacon."

"That's great, and I am sure you were hungry for a good meal. You look like you feel rested. I want to ask you a few questions if you don't mind. It will help us in our investigation of who abducted you and kept you for so long. Are you up to a few questions?"

"I sure am. Anything to help."

"Okay, I will record our conversation to have everything accurate. Is that okay with you?"

"Yes, although I am only thirteen, am I too young?"

"It is fine. This is a criminal investigation, and you're not the criminal."

"What is the first thing you remember after getting abducted? Do you remember any smells, music, noise, or anything unusual besides that you were being held against your will? Did they hit you or try to do anything of a sexual nature?"

"I just remember going to the bathroom at the mall. When I went into the stall, I got knocked up against the back wall, and someone stuck a needle in my right thigh. After that, I don't remember anything until I woke up in some basement with soundproofing material on the walls. It was gross, and it stunk like mold. I think it was two men, and that was all that had me in the beginning. They tried getting me to eat, but I refused food or water. I kicked at them even though they had my legs tied together. My arm was secured to the bedpost. It was an iron bedpost.

The bed stunk. The sheets were old and gross. I think they were blue, but I was so drugged I can't remember. I escaped once when I kept a fork they didn't realize I had, and one of them came down. When he opened the door, I stabbed him in the eye. I don't know if I blinded him, but I was trying to. I flew out of the room and found the door to get out, but the second guy had come down the stairs, and he caught me and gave me another shot, so I passed out again."

"That is great information, Lisa. You are doing great. I am sorry you are having to relive this."

"I don't mind if it will help catch these monsters."

Eliza knew that was a 'tell'. Lisa needed psychological help to overcome this, so she stopped the questioning.

"Thank you, Lisa. I think that is enough for now. I don't want to overtax you. I will call your mother and father and let them know I was here."

Trent and Michelle walked into the room just at that moment. Eliza stood and shook both of their hands.

"Lisa and I have been talking about her experience. I recorded our conversation. She has a great memory but needs to rest for a while. Is she being discharged today?"

"Yes, we have come to take her home," said Michelle.

"Great. May I speak with both of you in the hallway for a moment?"

"Yes, of course," Trent said. We'll be right back, baby," he told Lisa.

They all walked into the hallway away from Lisa's earshot. "I believe Lisa is going to need some therapy; the sooner, the better," said Eliza.

"We were planning on getting her started. The social worker gave us some names to call today. Is there anything else we should know?" asked Michelle.

"No, not really. I just heard her mention that the people who had her were monsters, and she is willing to do anything to help get them. She seemed very angry, which was a natural reaction initially. I would want her to focus her energies on getting over a traumatic event and for her to become a sweet little girl and not have vengeance in her heart. Do you know what I am saying?"

Michelle and Trent both nodded their agreement. "We understand, even though it is going to be a traumatic event she probably won't ever forget; hopefully, she will be able to get past it and not be distrustful of people for the rest of her life."

"Good, we are on the same page. I'm glad you understand," said

Eliza. "I will call tomorrow and make arrangements to talk with her again. Let her rest today. If possible, try not to let her speak with her friends. Her story needs to be kept close. She will have to be in a court-house one day, so please let her know how serious this is. Okay?"

"Yes, we understand, and thank you for your advice. See you tomor-row," said Trent.

Eliza stuck her head in Lisa's room and told her she would see her tomorrow morning and for her to get some rest today.

Lisa told her she would.

chapter

52

Jeffrey Edwards was all alone on his wife's yacht. He knew he was a wanted man. He had a television onboard, and he watched it last night. The local station was reporting the shooting and the rescue of the girl. His name hadn't been mentioned yet, but he was sure they knew he was in evolved by now.

He thought of going south but knew that was where they would first be looking. He decided to head north. He planned to find a port where he could leave the yacht, get a car, and head for Canada. He had the forethought of having a fake passport and driver's license made a few years ago. He never knew if he might need it. Especially since he and Britt started this venture, he wondered if Britt was scared and waiting for the Feds to arrive at his doorstep. He had no paper trail leading to him, so he should have no reason to worry. Jeffrey was a lot of things, but he was not a snitch.

Besides, he will get away unscathed if he plays his cards right. He had socked away money in a bank account in the Bahamas. He can access it from anywhere. It was enough so that he could live very comfortably for the rest of his life. He was sure the FBI would be on his computers and would find other sources of financial accounts, but they wouldn't see this one. He went through the proper channels and was sure he had secured the account. The U.S. government cannot access offshore accounts. He had a big smile when he thought of the anguish Stella was being put through. He almost, but not entirely, felt sorry for her.

He put the yacht in idle and went below to grab a beer and a sandwich he had made this morning. He's now glad he planned for any event. He sat down at the table made of mahogany and enjoyed the roast beef and provolone sandwich. He passed on chips for now. He wanted to stay trim and fit for any future romantic partner he might find. He would have to get used to being called Carl, the name on his passport, Carl Thurmond. It had a classy ring to it.

They were so close, but then Vera had to have a breakdown. Gil, being the lily-livered person he was, took up for his wife, and that was what got them both shot. He felt terrible for them. He had never shot a person before and didn't think he had it in him. He wasn't sure why he took the gun; it was a last-minute decision.

When he picked it up and placed it in his pocket, it made him feel dirty. He wasn't the violent type. He disapproved of hitting women or children. He wasn't brought up that way and wasn't sure what came over him. As he thought back, he believed he was just weary, and when Vera said she wouldn't go any farther, it triggered something in him. He remembered he had the gun, and he pulled it out. It was like he was watching a movie, but the difference was that he was the star.

He finished his sandwich and was getting the table cleaned up before grabbing a second beer and proceeding back up to the cockpit. When he reached the top, he heard the words he dreaded: "Put your hands up and get down on your knees."

Three Coast Guard Cutters surrounded the yacht, with at least ten guns pointed in his direction. Some were rifles, but most had standard-issued Glock pistols.

Jeffrey slowly put his left arm up, took his beer, showed it to them, and set it on the console. He then put his right arm up and got on his knees. The leader used a microphone and told him to lie in a prone position and keep his arms above his head. He did what they told him. Before he could get comfortable, there were three on his deck, and they put handcuffs on him and then stood him up. Another man walked up, took the steering wheel, and initiated driving the yacht. They carried him to the saloon, sat him down, and handcuffed him to the rail behind him.

They didn't start a conversation, and neither did Jeffrey. *Shit* was all he could think.

chapter

53

Stella Edwards was waiting for the attorney. She called her sister, Alice, and got her husband to find the best one in Raleigh. She couldn't wait to unload everything. She was more than mad that they tore her house up, then took her in, claiming it was for her own good. The food was awful, and she was starved.

An officer came to her cell and unlocked it. "Mrs. Edwards, come with me."

She followed the officer, and they entered a room where her attorney was waiting. She was a lovely African-American woman named Latrice Morgan. "I am here for support, Mrs. Edwards. Sheriff Taylor told me that your husband had been found as I walked in. There are no charges against you, and you are free to go. I won't be sending you a bill; this is non-grata. Please recommend me if you get a chance; here is my card. I am located in Raleigh."

Stella asked her, "Do you handle divorces?"

"Yes, call me."

With that, Ms. Morgan opened the door for Stella, and they walked to the front of the station. Stella waited for her purse, and she went through it and accepted that everything was there, so she signed the paperwork to get it back.

Sheriff Taylor approached her and took her hand. "I am sorry to have put you through all of this, Mrs. Edwards."

She stopped him and said, "I will be divorcing my husband ASAP, so please call me Stella."

"Okay, Stella. We were sincerely worried about your welfare because we knew he had a gun, and he could have come and held you hostage or several other scenarios I could see happen. None of them were good. I hope you understand and will not hold any bad feelings toward us here in Blaylock County."

She softened and said, "I understand and am pleased Lisa Williams has been found. Where is my husband?"

"The Coast Guard caught him, and he is on his way back to the New Bern port, where he will be met by the two FBI agents and brought back to Blaylock County. You are safe and are allowed to go home. I will have my officer drive you if that is okay?"

"I would prefer to arrange my transport. Could you please get Cynthia Curtis on the phone for me?" asked Stella.

"It would be my pleasure," said Kellum. "Wait in the lobby, and I will get her for you."

It was only a few minutes, and Sheriff Taylor brought his cell phone to Stella. She spoke with Cynthia Curtis for a short time and then handed the phone back to Kellum. "She will be here in half an hour to take me home. Thank you, Sheriff."

chapter

54

Eliza and Jay were waiting at the Coast Guard station in Wilmington when the Cutter carrying the passenger came into view. They let out a long-held sigh of relief.

Captain Garramone exited and introduced himself to the Agents. "We were able to capture your suspect without incident. He hasn't made a statement of any kind. He only asked to go to the bathroom once, and my Lieutenant accompanied him. He was uncuffed briefly, but there was no resistance when re-cuffed. Do you have any questions?"

"No sir," said Jay, and Eliza nodded in agreement.

Jeffrey was brought up from the saloon, taken to the nearest exit, and assisted onto the dock. He kept his head down. His clothes looked dirty and tattered. He wore jeans, a golf shirt, and a white nylon jacket. His blond streaked hair was messy. He had not combed it. It looked like he had not shaved for several days or more.

As he climbed onto the dock, he stumbled but caught himself and stood up straight. That was when he looked at Jay and Eliza. He recognized them and nodded but kept mute. Jay replaced the Coast Guard cuffs with his own. He read him his Miranda rights, and they walked toward the parking lot. Captain Garramone caught up with them and had Eliza sign several documents to complete the transfer. They put Jeffrey in the backseat, and Jay climbed in beside him. By this time, he had also used shackles given to him by Captain Garramone and shackled his legs out of precaution. Eliza drove to Murray in silence.

Once at the Sheriff's office, they noticed the number of media trucks out front. They could not avoid them, so Eliza called the Sheriff and told him they had arrived. Kellum told her to pull up in the designated space where he would park and be right out to help. She did as he said, and when they got Jeffrey out of the car, the media converged on them like locusts. With Eliza's assistance, Kellum got Jeffrey into the station, and Turner was there to start the booking process. Kellum went back out front to deal with the media.

He told them to back up and that he would hold an ad hoc news conference, which he did.

"We were able to apprehend Jeffrey Edwards, the primary suspect in the abduction of Lisa Williams. Everything that was given to you at this morning's conference is the same. The Coast Guard out of Wilmington was responsible for the apprehension. I understand that other units assisted them, and we are happy they could capture the suspect without incident."

"Was there anyone else with him?" asked the CNN reporter.

"At this time, I only know of Mr. Edwards. I don't believe there was anyone with him."

"Did he admit to the abduction?" asked Anthony Allen from WRAL-TV.

"I don't have any information about that, but the FBI agents will interview him shortly. Now, you know everything I know. I will keep you informed if any news breaks."

Kellum turned and walked into the station. He heard the noise outside and knew they were packing for the day. He hoped he could get home for dinner tonight. It had been a long couple of weeks. He smiled at the thought. He pulled out his cell phone and called Shannon. When she answered, he said, "What's for dinner?"

EPILOGUE

The following June, Jeffrey Edwards was tried for the conspiracy and abduction of Lisa Williams. He was found guilty on all counts, of which there were many. He was sentenced to Life plus Thirty years.

In a second trial that took place a month later, he was found guilty of second-degree murder in the death of Vera Gardner and the attempted murder of Gil Gardner. He was given the sentence of life plus twenty-five years.

He never mentioned his partner in crime, Britt. He made a conscious decision not to be a snitch. No one knew about Britt's involvement, so why mess up another life? After all, he was a husband and father. His brother, Christian, had been seriously injured in a car accident while driving to meet Jeffrey, but he had recovered and was back at work. He hoped that somewhere down the road, he would be forgiven, and he wanted to pay it forward now.

He was in Bahama, NC, at the Butner Federal Pron, the same prison Bernie Madoff served until he died in 2021. Jeffrey thought that was fitting since he was a hedge fund manager but thought he was better than Bernie. His clients never lost money.

His company absorbed his client's business and dispensed it to other managers. Most stayed with them, but some had their scruples and left to go with another firm. He hoped they were all being taken care of. Making money for clients was probably the best thing he had done all his life.

Stella Bernstock divorced her husband as quickly as NC law allowed. She became friends with Cynthia Curtis and also an advocate in her own right by becoming involved in human trafficking, especially children. She also became a philanthropist for causes that she found near and dear. She followed the political scene, and after her divorce, she began dating again. She was currently being seen with a very eligible U. S. Senator, but they were trying to keep their courtship quiet. Stella doesn't ever want to be married to a philanderer again. She was ready to settle down with someone who loved her and would like a family.

Walter Green was charged with kidnapping, but since he turned himself in and cooperated, his attorney negotiated a lighter sentence: five years in prison and twenty-five years of probation. He was required to complete five hundred hours of community service after he was released. His wife supported him and promised to be there when he was released.

Vinnie was never found, and they had no information about him. Jeffrey refused to cooperate, stating he didn't know Vinnie's last name, but the DA didn't believe him. Vinnie was in the wind, and he skated. So did the two guys, supposedly brothers, who were the middlemen in the abduction.

Gil Gardner fully recovered and had an attorney assigned to him because he claimed to be indigent. The home he lived in belonged to Jeffrey Edwards. His wife had been retired from nursing for many years. It came out in court records that she had been let go for diverting narcotics. She was able to go through a program to get clean, but she couldn't regain her nursing license, so she never returned to work as an RN. They were scraping by on whatever work Gil could get selling scrap metal, and she did a few private duty jobs occasionally. Gil went to prison for several charges surrounding the abduction of Lisa Williams, the worst being conspiracy of human trafficking. He received a thirty-year sentence with a chance for parole after fifteen. He also went to Butner Prison.

Katarina Kennedy (not her real name, for obvious reasons) continued as an FBI asset, but she stopped the sex work. The FBI had sent her to their facility in Colorado to learn more about how to prevent and apprehend internet child pornographers. She made a deal with them, though. She insisted she had to go to New York every December for Christmas.

Brent Williams was accepted at NC State and prepared to start in the fall. Angela got a small scholarship through the Arts Council, so she will join him there. She planned to major in Art and hoped to become a graphic artist. Ken Harper, her stepdad, said he would help pay for her dormitory expenses. He had already placed five thousand in an account for her to use at school. She and Brent still planned to marry and discussed doing it after their sophomore year.

Brenda, Angela's mother, was still at the restaurant but had been able to cut her hours to be home with Andy in the afternoon. Her neighbor, Jim Montgomery, had been a constant visitor at their home, and Angela liked him. He was a good influence on her mother, and Andy looked up to him. Angela wondered if he may ask her mother to marry him soon. It was apparent on both their faces that they were crazy about each other. That pleased Angela. She was going to miss Andy, but he would be in school this fall so that he would keep him busy, and she promised she would call him almost every day. He laughed and told her, "Bet you, you won't." She knew he was probably right. She was going to be busy, too.

Lisa Williams had matured so much since her abduction. She attended both trials and was engrossed in their legal aspects. She couldn't get enough of sitting with the prosecutors and watching them work. Her mother and father indulged her every whim. They were happy to know she was at home and not a statistic. Michelle started listening to some podcasts on true crime, and it was so astonishing how many people, especially children, go missing every year. It had become a passion of hers. She tried to get Trent to listen, but he was still too emotional and unprepared to put himself through anything like that.

Eliza returned to work at Three Island Catering two weeks after Lisa's recovery. She met with Gene and told him all she could, but she had to leave out certain things that would come out during the trial. Gene seemed relieved to have her back. "The business had picked up due to our superb reputation," he smiled. "I'm not complaining; you understand?"

"Yes, I understand. My secret is safe?"

"It certainly is. I'm supposed to see my cousin this fall, and I will have to train myself not to flinch if he mentions your name," he burst out laughing, and so did Eliza.

About the Author

E. L. Boyer is a retired RN. She grew up in Atlanta, Georgia, before moving to Ohio. After living in Ohio for ten years, she and her husband, Larry, moved to coastal NC, and she retired a few years later. She loves to golf and play Mah Jongg, but mostly, she loves to read.

Her first fictional book, A Measure of Kindness, introduced the characters of Ally Malcom and her friend Mary Hughes. She enjoys listening to true crime podcasts which focuses on missing persons. Her two favorites are *Going West* and *Murder With My Husband*.

She continues to battle the syndrome known as Burning Mouth. It is an incurable condition. It is a rare thing and plagues people worldwide. She continues to pray that there may be a cure one day.

She encourages the readers to send the names and types of pets they have so she can continue to introduce them in future books.

You can reach her at liz@elboyer.com as well as her website, www.boyersbookshelf.com

Please remember to review on Amazon or any other place you prefer. Also please Follow her on Amazon's Author Page.

Other books by the author are A Measure of Kindness and A Lie More Real Than Truth.